OPPOSING THE COWBOY

A HOMETOWN HEROES NOVEL

MARGO BOND COLLINS

Entangled Publishing, LLC
2614 South Timberline Road
Suite 109
Fort Collins, CO 80525
Visit our website at www.entangledpublishing.com.

Bliss is an imprint of Entangled Publishing, LLC. For more information on our titles, visit http://www.entangledpublishing.com/category/bliss

Edited by Alycia Tornetta
Cover design by Jessica Cantor
Cover art from iStock

Manufactured in the United States of America

First Edition July 2015

Bliss
An Entangled Imprint

This book is dedicated to the Blazing Indies. I couldn't manage without y'all!

Chapter One

What an ass-hat.

LeeAnn Walker pushed herself up onto her hands and feet, leaning into downward dog until she felt the stretch across the backs of her calves. She tried to concentrate on perfecting the pose in an attempt to push the memory of the previous night's teary phone call out of her mind.

I can't believe Darrell cheated on me.

Angie, the instructor, called out directions in a soothing voice. "Push up onto your toes, then slide your torso along the ground and between your arms."

Pay attention, LeeAnn.

Shifting into cobra, she shook several loose tendrils of blond hair out of her eyes and arched her back enough to glance up at the wall clock.

If we wrap up in the next ten minutes, I should have time to take a quick shower and grab breakfast at the new diner. What's it called? Wagon Yard? Chuck Wagon? Something like that.

"Back up to down dog," Angie intoned.

Damn Darrell all the way to hell and back.

The two-timing bastard. I can't believe he's marrying someone else.

Time to rein those thoughts back in. Bursting into tears in the middle of yoga class would defeat the purpose of the exercises, right?

Breathe.

Stretch.

There were lots of things about her life that were great. She had good friends.

Her part-time job working at Cowbelles, her best friend Kylie's gift shop, covered her immediate expenses.

She was getting better and better as a yoga teacher and had almost finished her instructor's certification—in only two or three months, she would be able to run any class TexZen offered. Hopefully, the studio would give her a full-time position.

So it doesn't matter if Darrell Cheating Jerkwad Vincent broke up with me to marry someone else.

I am calm and centered.

Yeah. Right.

Follow Angie's instructions.

Move. Don't think.

She closed her eyes and leaned back on her mat, though she certainly wasn't in the right frame of mind for the meditation session that ended the class.

At the front of the room, Angie crossed her legs lotus style. "Om," she intoned, holding her thumbs and forefingers together.

LeeAnn blew out a sigh, then crossed her legs and joined the chant.

Nama-freaking-ste.

• • •

LeeAnn Walker.

Reaching into the battered leather bag on the seat beside him in his green '56 Chevy, Jonah Hamilton pulled out a file and flipped through the pages.

He needed to know more.

She wasn't the first person who'd refused to let Natural Shale Oil and Gas drill on their land. But this was the first time he hadn't been able to figure out why.

Driving past her ranch this morning and staring over the fence at the property he so desperately needed access to hadn't given him any new insights, either.

It's not like she can't use the money.

The house and main barn seemed sturdy enough, though they needed a coat or two of paint—but the outbuildings were practically falling in on themselves. And looking at the state of the boundary markers made him itch to saddle up and ride the fences.

When he'd spoken to the woman on the phone the first time two months ago, she'd been polite, but firm, in her refusal to meet with him.

By last week she'd been downright hostile, even going so far as to hang up on him midsentence.

But every survey that Natural Shale had done suggested that her land was the perfect place to drill. And as the company's landman, it was his job to arrange for drilling access.

Jonah Hamilton did not fail. That's why the company had put him on the job. He always got what he wanted, what the company wanted, in the end, no matter how much the landowner initially protested.

LeeAnn Walker was no different.

Time to do a little research, and then apply some in-person charm.

But first, breakfast.

Grabbing the well-worn Stetson from the passenger seat and settling it on his head, he slid out of the truck and headed into the diner.

. . .

As she walked out of the studio, LeeAnn's stomach rumbled at the smell of bacon frying. Even as she reminded herself that vegetarians shouldn't crave pork products, she followed the smell around the corner to the diner that had only recently opened.

WAGON WHEEL DINER, she read on the sign as she drew nearer. She glanced at her watch.

Half an hour ought to give me enough time to grab breakfast and still open Cowbelles on time. I can stick to pancakes.

Of course, she hadn't counted on the line of people snaking up to the order counter. She should have known better—anyplace new was bound to be even more crowded than the usual Stockyards District restaurants, and few places served breakfast.

Shifting from one foot to the other, she checked her watch, then froze as a familiar laugh drifted through the restaurant. Her gaze followed the sound back to its origin.

Darrell Jerkwit Cheater Vincent.

Sitting right there at a table with a group of businessmen, as if he had every right to smile and laugh and act as if he weren't a despicable example of humanity.

Jerk.

Her stomach clenched. It wasn't like Fort Worth was a small town, even if working in the Stockyards District sometimes made it seem as if it were. She had options. She didn't have to stick around.

In fact, it would be better if she got out of here before he saw her at all.

Dick.

She spun on her heel to march out the door and smacked into a muscled wall of masculine chest—then bounced right back off, her arms pinwheeling for a moment, before the toe of her sneaker caught on a chair and she landed flat on her butt on the hard, ceramic tile floor.

As if the impact had knocked it out of her, her next thought about Darrell popped out of her mouth in a breathy whoosh as she landed.

"Man slut."

"Pardon me?" Although the collision had rocked him back on his boot heels a little, the man she had careened off seemed otherwise unaffected as he held out his hand to help her up.

The guy looming over her reminded LeeAnn of someone, though she couldn't figure out who.

Maybe an actor or a model? He's that hot.

Part of her realized that her stare was turning rude, but she couldn't seem to help herself. And he knew exactly what effect he was having on her—she could see it in the way his deep, dark blue eyes sparkled in amusement. His hair matched his eyes—it was a black so deep that it seemed to have blue highlights.

A cleft chin that movie stars would kill for.

And a muscular chest that a girl could bounce right off.

"Like Superman comics," she whispered.

"Are you okay?" He leaned in closer and reached out with both hands as if to steady her as she scrambled up.

No ring, she noted. *Not that I care.*

"I'm fine." LeeAnn backed away. "Sorry about that."

Everyone in the Wagon Wheel was staring at her now. Although she wanted to, she didn't risk looking at Darrell. Bad enough he had dumped her. She couldn't bear the thought of him watching her as she made a fool out of herself.

The burn of a deep flush crept up her neck, then flashed across her cheeks.

"Excuse me," she whispered, brushing past the gorgeous man who was now blocking the exit.

"Really, are you okay?" the beautiful man said, once again reaching out as if to touch her shoulder.

She froze for the barest instant, then turned her head just far enough to look into those navy blue eyes.

Almost against her will, her gaze flicked back toward Darrell.

He was watching, but he was far enough away that he almost certainly hadn't heard their conversation.

And the sneaky, lying, cheating son of a bitch was smirking.

Swinging back around to fully face the man in the doorway, she acted on impulse. She might not know who this amazing, beautiful, Superman-looking guy was, but in that instant, she didn't care.

Maybe she could, for a moment, show Darrell...something.

This is probably a bad idea.

She ignored the tiny voice in the back of her head.

"Work with me," she whispered to the man in front of her.

He had only a second for a confused look to flicker across his face before she stood up on her tiptoes, wrapped her arms around his neck, threaded her fingers through the silky hair just brushing the nape of his neck, and pulled him down to kiss her.

It took one interminable heartbeat for him to respond, long enough for LeeAnn to realize that this might have been the worst idea she'd ever had.

Or maybe the second worst idea, right after Darrell.

And then he took over.

Arms banded with muscles circled her waist, crushing her against that unbelievably broad chest. His tongue teased at her lips, and she found herself melting into him for a long, blissful moment.

When he finally pulled away gently, setting her feet back on the ground, she blinked. Slowly, she unwrapped her arms from around his neck, breathless and dazed.

"Let's skip breakfast," he said in a suggestive tone, loud enough to be heard through the suddenly silent diner.

"O-okay," she stammered, following as he tugged her out the door.

As they stepped outside into the bright morning sunlight and the glass door swung closed behind them, LeeAnn tried to gather her senses, still reeling from that kiss.

The Superman look-alike blocked her view of the booths inside the Wagon Wheel.

Just as well. The last thing she wanted was to see Darrell's smug face. Still, she found herself peeking around the stranger's broad shoulders to peer in the window.

All she saw was her own reflection.

"I'm guessing that was for someone else's benefit?" His deep voice drew her attention back to him, her glance snagging on his mischievous grin.

Dear God, he's got dimples, too.

"Yes," she said, finally dragging her gaze from his smile and up far enough to make eye contact.

"Then I'm happy to help." He tilted his head and touched the brim of his hat. With a glance at the window, he offered her his arm. "Walk with me as far as the lot?" he asked, a gleam in his eyes. "We don't want your audience seeing us part ways here."

What had she been thinking?

It was all Darrell's fault. What had he been doing there? He didn't even work in the Stockyards District. This was supposed to be her part of town. He was supposed to stay out of it.

Not that he ever did what he was supposed to.

That was at the heart of their problem, wasn't it?

"Bastard," she muttered. Straightening her spine, she took a deep breath and wrapped her hand around the stranger's arm.

"Is there a reason you keep calling me names?" he

asked, falling into step beside her.

Because I'm clearly losing my mind?

"Oh, no. I'm sorry. I didn't mean you." A quick glance up at him told her he was still smiling—and listening, if a little too intently for her taste. "My ex was in there. I didn't want to see him. The name-calling was about him."

"Bad breakup, I take it." Somehow his tone managed to be both bland and sympathetic.

"The worst." She stopped in the middle of the parking lot. "I'm sorry. I don't even know why I'm talking about this."

And no one in the Wagon Wheel can see us anymore.

She unwound her arm from his.

"Anyway, thanks," she said.

"For the assist back there? Sure. Anytime." Amusement colored his deep voice. "This one's mine," he said, motioning toward a pickup—an old one, but so well cared for that it looked practically new.

The same kind Granddad used to drive.

She nodded, taking a step back as he unlocked the door. "Okay. Thanks again."

Laughing a little, he swung up into the Chevy and gave a little two-fingered salute, touching the brim of his hat.

LeeAnn watched as he drove out of the parking lot.

I could spend all day watching his ass slide onto that bench seat.

I didn't even get his name.

• • •

Irritation warred with amusement as Jonah pulled out of the Starbucks drive-through ten minutes later.

I should have gotten her name. Or bought her coffee, at least.

Or maybe something more.

The memory of that kiss burned on his lips, and he shifted in his seat. The way she had molded herself to him, the slight flare of her hip filling his hand, her breasts crushed against his chest—all of it, perfect. When she had blushed, he had wanted to wrap her in his arms again.

Whoever dumped her is an idiot.

No, I'm an idiot for not finding out who she is.

But her ex was having breakfast in the same diner she frequented. Maybe she was a local?

So he would…what? Hang out at the Wagon Wheel every morning until she showed up?

Yeah, I'm definitely an idiot.

He had too much work to do to worry about one kiss from a stranger.

Shaking his head, he took a long pull from the coffee and turned left onto Throckmorton Street. He'd tracked down everything he could about Lee Ann Walker's property online, but it still hadn't helped him figure out why she was refusing Natural Shale's offer. Maybe some time in the Tarrant County records office would yield better results.

Either way, this afternoon he would stop by the gift store where she worked and see what he could glean from talking to her in person.

This deal was the final step to a promotion to senior landman. It didn't matter how many times he told himself he didn't need the money—that he wasn't his father, jobless and hopeless, dependent upon his children to support him in his angry old age. Every move forward in his career made

Jonah feel stronger.

He always won. And he would win this time, too.

LeeAnn Walker didn't stand a chance. She'd never know what hit her.

Time to go deal with the rude chick from hell.

But he'd keep an eye out for his beautiful stranger in the meantime.

Chapter Two

By noon, LeeAnn was starving.

That's what I get for skipping breakfast in favor of kissing a stranger.

But it was one hell of a kiss.

She shook herself to keep from slipping back into another daydream about it.

Dreamy. That's a good word for him.

With a rumble, her stomach reminded her of more pressing concerns.

Right. Lunch.

Usually she brown-bagged it, but she'd been too exhausted from reliving the breakup over and over again all night to do more than drag herself to yoga class that morning.

There were a few places in the Stockyards that delivered, but none of them had good vegetarian options, and she was sick of salads.

She debated leaving long enough to pick something

up. Even though she knew Kylie often closed the shop for lunch, LeeAnn hesitated. She didn't want to miss any sales. Keeping Cowbelles going while Kylie was gone mattered to her—and not only because she was getting paid. It would be nice to be able to relieve all of her friend's anxieties about leaving town. The more sales LeeAnn made, the happier Kylie would be when she returned at the end of the week from her monthlong trip touring with Cole Grayson, her country music star boyfriend.

But if I don't eat lunch, I'll get cranky and end up running customers away.

With a sigh, she hung the BE RIGHT BACK sign on the door and spun the hands on the paper clock around to twelve thirty.

As she moved toward the stockroom to grab her purse, though, the electronic chimes over the door jingled, letting her know someone had come in.

Closing her eyes briefly—long enough to send up a short prayer requesting the patience to deal with whoever had ignored the sign—LeeAnn pasted a bright smile on her face and spun to greet the customer.

The smile froze in place as she made eye contact with the man standing inside as the door swung closed behind him.

The guy from the Wagon Wheel.

Superman in a cowboy hat.

And from the poleaxed look on his face, he hadn't expected her any more than she expected him—despite the next words out of his mouth.

"I'm looking for LeeAnn Walker."

In the long silence that followed, the two blinked at one

another.

I'm staring again.

"I'm LeeAnn," she said.

And now he's the one staring.

What is going on here?

"So, Clark Kent," LeeAnn said, finally breaking the long silence. "How do you know my name?"

"Clark Kent?" His startled laugh was low and full and went straight to her abdomen. When she didn't answer, he continued. "I'm Jonah Hamilton."

Superman of kisses.

Not that she would say that out loud.

Not on purpose, anyway.

Even without an audience, the impulse to kiss him hadn't faded. Her cheeks heated at the memory.

Jonah Hamilton. Where have I heard that name before?

"Can I help you with something?" she asked.

He gestured at the sign on the door. "Were you about to head out for lunch?"

"You didn't answer my question. How do you know my name?" Her stomach dropped in sudden, irrational fear. "Are you following me? Are you stalking me or something?"

There's that laugh again.

"You're the one who kissed me, remember?" Jonah's dimples flashed as he spoke.

Oh, if only I could forget.

"Can we go somewhere and sit down? Maybe for coffee, if you don't want lunch?" He tilted his head, regarding her steadily as he waited for her answer.

Some part of her brain noted that he had a practiced smile that made her a little nervous—and a mischievous gleam in his eye that made her pulse race.

"I really don't have time—I need to get back to work." And fresh off a breakup, the last thing she needed was to spend time with this gorgeous, blue-eyed temptation to rebound.

Ignore the beautiful man.

Be calm.

Centered.

Definitely time to practice some yoga-style pranayama breathing.

Counting silently, she drew in a deep, slow breath through her nose, then blew it out through her mouth.

She could almost hear Angie's voice in her mind.

Exhales should be twice as long as inhales. One, two, three. One, two, three, four, five, six. One, two—

"What are you doing?" Jonah asked.

LeeAnn placed her hands in prayer position at heart level. "Breathing," she said.

—three, four, five, six.

There. That's better.

Stretching her hands high above her head, then circling her arms wide as she brought them down to her sides, Lee-Ann came to rest in mountain pose.

Feet planted in the earth, the crown of my head stretching to the sky.

I am calm.

I am centered.

I can deal with this man.

I can deal with anything.

"Now," she said, focusing on keeping her voice low and melodic to reflect the calm she wanted to create in the room, "how can I help you?"

"Is this some sort of joke?" Jonah's gaze darted around the store, taking in the rhinestone- and cowhide-covered trinkets, the barbed-wire crosses hanging on the walls, the melamine-encased bluebonnets attached to key chains.

Texas kitsch. Tourist crap. Normal enough for the Stockyards District.

Nothing about the place suggested that it was staffed by a crazy woman who did weird breathing exercises while she prayed.

And handed out stunning kisses to strangers at the local diner.

"Is there a camera somewhere?" he asked.

A display on the far left wall entitled "Hometown Heroes" drew Jonah's attention. An oversize poster version of the cover of country singer Cole Grayson's latest album took up most of the space. Smaller images of a bull rider surrounded it. Less explicably, what looked like a few shreds of an old concert poster were tacked to the wall next to Grayson's image, their tattered strands fluttering in the slight breeze of the air conditioner.

He zeroed in on what looked like a security camera. "Seriously—am I being punked?"

Placing her hands back in their prayer position, Lee-Ann—*if that's really who she is*—raised one eyebrow as she lifted her right foot and set it on the inside of her thigh.

"Punked?" she asked, her warm alto voice rising a bit.

"Yeah. You know, like *Candid Camera*." He bent down

a bit to peer at the underside of the camera. It did seem to be plugged in.

"No. You're not being punked." She balanced on one foot, like a crane.

A beautiful, graceful crane with the most amazing kisses.

Blinking rapidly to dispel the rather disturbing image, Jonah took his own deep breath and stood up straight again.

Whatever was going on here, he needed to take control of the situation. "Let's start over," he said.

"Okay." LeeAnn tilted her head a little to one side but didn't change her one-legged prayer-hands stance.

He pulled out his wallet and held out a business card. "My name is Jonah Hamilton. I represent Natural Shale Oil and Gas, the company that is looking to drill on your ranch."

LeeAnn froze, one hand reaching halfway across the distance separating them, the other still at her heart in prayer position.

"Absolutely not," she said. Her upraised foot finally dropped to the ground. Her gray eyes darkened, matching her suddenly chilly tone. "Jonah Hamilton. You're the one who's been calling me."

Ah. There's the ice queen I've been talking to.

He nodded, careful not to let his thoughts show on his face. "Yes, ma'am."

Pursing her lips, she moved behind the sales counter, putting both distance and a barrier between them.

Reading body language during negotiations—normal body language, not some weird-ass, twisty praying shit—*now* he was in his element.

"I told you over the phone. I will never allow anyone to drill on my land." She crossed her arms over her chest.

Still holding out the card, Jonah shrugged. "You may not have any say in it."

"It's *my* land," she said. Her lips thinned as she spoke, her nostrils flaring a bit. "My decision is final."

He leaned forward far enough to place his card on the counter in front of her. "We may be able to drill on the property whether you like it or not. That's what I'm in town to find out."

Her eyes widened, and her mouth opened as if to speak, but no sound came out.

Tell her about the letter now?

No. Best to leave before she regained her equilibrium.

Taking one step back, he tilted his head and touched the brim of his hat. "I'll be in touch, Ms. Walker." Then he turned and left the store, the electronic bells jingling into the silence behind him.

Not until he was sitting in his truck again did he take off his hat and blow out a deep breath.

Holy shit.

The ice queen of Fort Worth and the most sensuous woman I've ever kissed are the same person.

He stared out the window at the brick-paved streets.

While preparing for this particular contract, he'd spent all his time researching the land.

I need to research the woman.

A slow grin spread across his face.

I think I may be in trouble.

And I think it's going to be fun.

· · ·

LeeAnn stared at the card on the counter in front of her as if it were a rattlesnake poised to strike.

Finally, she reached out and picked it up between two fingers, staring at the Natural Shale logo across the top and Jonah's name beneath.

Its bite might be as poisonous as a rattler.

What had Jonah Hamilton meant, they might be able to drill even without her permission?

Surely he was lying.

And oh, dear Lord. I kissed *him this morning.*

With a groan, she dropped her forearms onto the counter and banged her head against the back of her hands several times.

The only other people who might know anything about the ranch were her cousins, Samantha and Beverly. She looked at the clock. Beverly was in California, finishing her master's degree in psychology—no telling if she would be available to talk. But Sami was probably still on her lunch break. If LeeAnn called right now, Sami might have time to talk to her.

With a sigh, LeeAnn pulled the sign from the door and went to the back room to get her cell phone.

Looks like I'm having a salad delivered again.

"I don't know anything about mineral rights." Her cousin Sami's voice came through a bit muffled as LeeAnn balanced the phone between her shoulder and her ear so she could pluck a T-shirt from the jumble on the shelf and refold it.

Sami continued talking. "All I know is that the money

went to Daddy and the land was willed to your mom, then after she died, to you. I haven't even looked at those papers since Daddy died—it's not like there was anything left for me or Bev once he got his hands on it."

LeeAnn made a sympathetic noise. "But you still have the paperwork?"

"I have no idea. I think it might still be out at the ranch—Gran had us bring everything that looked important over there after his funeral. Maybe it's in the attic, or out in one of the barns? I'm sorry. I wish I knew." The shrug in her cousin's voice came through clearly.

"Do you remember Gran talking about someone wanting to drill back in the eighties?" As determined as she had always been to keep the oil companies off her land, surely Gran would have said something to someone.

"Not really—but she talked to you about that stuff more than me, so it's no surprise that I wouldn't remember." LeeAnn heard a voice in the background—probably Sami's jerk of a boss, demanding she hang up. "Listen, I've got to get back to work. Can we talk later?"

"Okay. Thanks anyway." With a sigh, she swiped the off button. It had been a slim chance at best, so she wasn't really surprised that Sami couldn't help her.

She didn't know anything about mineral rights—nothing about oil companies except that they did terrible things to the land. Something about fracking. Even the word sounded bad. If she was really going to have to go up against some big oil company, she needed more information.

Guess I'm going to have to talk to this Jonah guy again, after all.

And ignore those dimples.

But above all, pretend I never, ever kissed him.

She stared down at the business card on the counter in front of her.

Contacting him wasn't going to be easy. The whole thing made her stomach hurt. Luckily, she knew just the stretch for that pain—she'd even cleared a spot in the middle of the store, exactly the size of her yoga mat.

Kylie won't mind. Right?

Stretching her arms up over her head, she leaned back farther and farther, until her hands touched the mat in a perfect back bend. Enjoying the stretch the pose created through her abdomen, she closed her eyes and concentrated on her breathing.

That's better.

She would have to deal with Jonah Hamilton and Natural Shale Oil and Gas soon enough. But in the midst of chaos, she could create an oasis of calm—even if it didn't extend any farther than her mat.

Tomorrow.

I will call the number on that card tomorrow.

Maybe.

Chapter Three

By the next afternoon, Jonah was pretty sure he had what he needed. He leaned back from the screen of the microfiche machine, squeezing the bridge of his nose and blinking. If anyone had told him in college that he would end up in a career that required him to do research on a regular basis — and more, that he would love that part of his job — he would have laughed his ass off. But here he sat, moving back and forth between the microfilm scans of the old archives and the screen of the laptop on the desk beside him. He loved the treasure hunt aspect of the research, finding the clues that led back to the records he needed, that took him to the land title, newspaper story, or even old diary that showed who owned the mineral rights to a piece of land.

Tracking down mineral rights might not always be simple or straightforward, but there was always an answer. It was a problem with a specific, definable solution.

Of course, he might not love the research quite as much

if he had to do it all the time. The fact that the other half of his job required him to work outside as much as inside made up for any difficulties he ran into when digging through old records.

And this time?

Pay dirt.

Between the county records and what he'd found in the library as he sorted through old newspaper reports, he'd put together a pretty clear picture of LeeAnn Walker's life, along with her connection to the land Natural Shale wanted to drill.

Orphaned when she was four, she had gone to live with her grandparents on what had then been a working ranch. When her grandfather died ten years later, her grandmother, an elementary school teacher in Fort Worth, hadn't been able to keep the ranch going by herself. Instead, she had given a cash inheritance to her only living son—LeeAnn's uncle, George. Then, in order to hang on to the land itself, she'd slowly sold off the animals and let go of the ranch hands, one by one. When the grandmother died and LeeAnn inherited the now defunct ranch, she had been forced to sell off the back twenty acres to pay the inheritance taxes.

In fact, she had apparently struggled to pay the property taxes ever since she inherited, sometimes incurring a hefty late fee and often arranging to pay them out over time. Jonah riffled through the photocopies of tax records he had added to the file.

Why didn't she take out a mortgage on the place? She could have arranged to have the taxes bundled into a monthly payment. Whatever her reasoning, it looked like she was in a bind now—she had about a month left before she would have to pay up again. And unless she had some income source other than the gift shop job and, apparently, a gig teaching a few classes each week at the yoga studio, he didn't think she was going to find it any easier to pay the tax bill this time.

But the whole yoga teacher thing certainly explained her reluctance to lease out the drilling rights. He'd run up against the type before—neo-hippie do-gooders, convinced they could change the world by chanting or some shit like that. They thought oil companies were out to destroy the world, and that they could save it.

Tree huggers and the like.

Usually smell like pot.

He drew up short at the thought. Lee Ann Walker hadn't smelled like that at all. She had smelled warm and clean, with a hint of vanilla.

Still, a yoga teacher who can't pay her taxes? Obviously a flake.

He glanced over at the screen of his laptop, taking in her smiling image. The picture in the *Fort Worth Star-Telegram* was from a charity event at the Will Rogers Coliseum. Any other time, someone like LeeAnn probably wouldn't have ended up with her picture in the paper, but she stood next to Cole Grayson in the photo, along with the famous country singer's girlfriend, Kylie Andrews—the woman who owned the gift shop where LeeAnn worked, he had discovered. On the other side of LeeAnn, another man stared off into the distance, unsmiling. LeeAnn held his arm, but his body language was unresponsive, his lips pressed together in a thin, angry line.

I'd bet anything that's the guy from the Wagon Wheel.

"Darrell Vincent," the caption read.

A wave of heat rolled through Jonah at the memory of LeeAnn's kiss.

What a colossal dumbass Darrell Vincent must be.

On a whim, Jonah pulled up his public data records account and ran a search on the guy, finding only the most basic of information: local address, no arrest record.

Next, he tried Google.

Salesman for a local business, participated in some small golf tournaments.

He scrolled down a bit.

Bingo.

An engagement announcement: Darrell Vincent and Margaret Carter. In yesterday's newspaper.

He switched tabs to look back at the picture with Grayson in it.

Not even six weeks ago.

If this guy was LeeAnn's bad breakup, he had sure moved on fast.

A quick search of the bride-to-be's background gave Jonah a pretty good answer for that. Margaret Carter was part of the Fort Worth elite, apparently—she came from old cattle money and was a successful attorney in her own right.

That painted a clear picture: the part-time salesclerk, part-time yoga instructor struggling to pay her land taxes dumped for the rich lawyer with connections.

What a prick. Jonah snarled at the thought, then paused.

What the hell are you doing, Hamilton?

This research was supposed to be about finding a way to convince LeeAnn to accept Natural Shale's drilling rights offer.

Not about figuring out her love life.

She had definitely gotten under his skin. With only one kiss?

One hot kiss.

Focus, Hamilton.

Right. How to get LeeAnn to accept the offer. Stick to business.

He stood up and stretched.

Time to go see her again.

• • •

When she rounded the corner on her way back to Cowbelles after lunch, the sight of the tall, broad-shouldered Superman look-alike leaning against the redbrick wall next to the door brought LeeAnn to a screeching halt.

Today he was dressed in cowboy professional: faded blue jeans that molded to the tops of his thighs, polished cowboy boots, a white button-down shirt, and a dark brown sport coat. His hat was tipped slightly down to shade his eyes, and his crossed arms pulled the jacket tight across his broad shoulders.

The sight of him sent a shiver down the back of LeeAnn's neck.

Jonah Hamilton.

I'm not ready to talk to him yet.

The cheese enchiladas she'd had at Azteca turned to a hard lump in her stomach.

Maybe he didn't see me.

As she took one slow step backward, though, he stood up straight and faced her, resettling his Stetson on his head and smiling.

I don't want to talk to him. Or even see him.

Except, oh, those dimples are beautiful.

And his lips…

The memory of the kiss in the Wagon Wheel felt burned into her skin, like he had branded her.

That's insane, LeeAnn. Get a grip.

Anyway. *Branded? I'm not a cow.*

Closing her eyes for an instant, she took a deep breath in, then blew it out, allowing a calming chant to run through her mind.

Om mani padme hum…

"Can I take that for you?" Jonah asked as he moved toward her, gesturing toward the Styrofoam box of leftovers she carried in her hand.

"Sure." She forced a polite smile and handed it over.

I am calm.

I am collected.

I am cool…

Damn, he's hot.

She pushed the stray thought away.

Om…

Unlocking the shop door and pulling it open, she motioned him inside.

"Ladies first," he said.

With a snort, she stepped into the dim interior and flipped the sign over to OPEN. He followed as she turned on lights and moved to the stockroom at the back of the store, where she took the box from him and bent over to place it in the small refrigerator.

When she turned around, he was leaning against the

doorjamb, his gaze pinned to the spot where her butt had just been. She ignored the blush crawling up her face, opting to simply raise her eyebrows instead.

His only response was an unrepentant grin.

"So," she said, pushing past him and moving back out into the display room, "how can I help you today?"

"I want to talk to you again about the mineral rights to your land." He leaned one elbow on a shelf and crossed his feet so that the tip of his right boot rested on the ground.

"No, thank you," she said. The polite smile she had held onto up to that point turned brittle, but she kept her voice calm. "I don't want you or your company anywhere near my land."

"The problem we're facing," he said, completely ignoring her attempt to shut him down, "is that I haven't been able to track down the actual mineral rights to your ranch."

"Doesn't sound like a problem to me," LeeAnn said. "That means they're mine."

"You think they're yours," he countered. "But you don't know for sure." Reaching into an inner pocket of his sport coat, he pulled out a folded paper. "You need to read this."

"What is it?" LeeAnn didn't wait for his answer, and when she unfolded it, she gasped.

Gran's handwriting.

Blinking back sudden, unexpected tears, she worked to make out the actual words. The paper was a photocopy of a single page, apparently a letter, though she couldn't tell who the recipient might have been. One line had been highlighted in neon-yellow marker: *"We will, of course, have to account for the mineral rights. They are currently in George's name, so—"* The letter ended in midsentence at the bottom of the page.

"What does this mean?" Her voice was scratchy with tears. She cleared her throat and waited for Jonah's response.

"It means that the lawyers who work for Natural Shale and Oil have at least some evidence that the drilling rights might not belong to you."

The image of trucks barreling across the ranch brought the tears she had suppressed moments ago flooding back into her eyes.

It wasn't only that she had promised Gran, over and over again in those last days, that she would take care of the ranch, keep it safe for future generations—although she had done exactly that. It wasn't even that she had protested the oil companies' recent increased drilling in the Permian Basin, although she'd done that, too, marching and holding placards, giving interviews to the journalists who showed up to cover the protest. And although she would tell anyone who asked that she didn't want her land destroyed by drilling, that she philosophically opposed all big oil companies, and that yogis should stand by their principles, on some level, she knew it went deeper than that.

She didn't have to figure it out right now, though.

To distract herself, she bit down hard on the inside of her cheek.

Breathe.

Om.

At the slightly puzzled expression on Jonah's face, she realized that she had bent one knee and pulled her foot up behind her into the crook of her elbow, all while balancing on the tip of the other toe.

Unconscious yoga practice can't be a good sign.

"The attorneys will be all over this." He held up one hand as she started to protest. "But I have a proposal."

A proposal?

She remembered the way his chest had felt against hers as he crushed her to him, his lips moving over hers as the kiss slowed and turned deeper.

That memory is dangerous.

Without her permission, LeeAnn's mind veered off into even more dangerous territory.

Oh, hell, no.

"Absolutely not," she said—more to herself than to him, but Jonah seemed taken aback by the vehemence in her voice.

"Hear me out," he said.

She narrowed her eyes at him but didn't reply.

Om…

"I meant it when I said you might not be able to keep us from drilling on your land—it might not be up to you," he said. "But I have a plan that might help both of us."

· · ·

LeeAnn's gray eyes turned dark and glinted at him. Clenching her jaw, she dropped down to stand on both feet, drawing a deep breath and steeling herself to speak. "I own the ranch. It's mine, and I say no one is going to drill on it. Do you know what damage that can do to the land?"

"There are perfectly safe drilling methods that won't do any permanent damage." He shook his head, as much to stop himself from speaking as to negate her statement. It wouldn't do any good to get drawn into defending the company's practices. This woman pulled him off center in a way no one ever had. "But that's not the point."

"You're right," she said. "The point is that the land is mine, and no one is drilling."

"Actually, the point is that you own the ranch, but you might not own the mineral rights." He gestured at the paper she clutched in one fist, then held out his hands placatingly. "Look. The truth is, I don't know who owns the mineral rights. Beyond that one letter, I haven't been able to find any records about them at all."

A tiny crinkle creased her forehead, and he fought the urge to smooth his thumb across it. "Is that unusual?" she asked.

He shrugged. "Not necessarily. The ranch has been in your family for generations, so it's possible that the kind of title transfers that would require that level of specificity simply haven't happened."

LeeAnn's gaze remained wary, and Jonah was pretty sure she was unaware that she had begun doing that strange crane stance again, lifting first one foot and placing it against her inner thigh and then switching out.

Yoga as a nervous habit?

One of the best tricks in a negotiation, he had learned over the years, was simply waiting silently. People tended to want to fill a silence. So Jonah watched as LeeAnn shifted from one foot to the other. The moment she realized what she doing, though, she planted both feet on the floor and stood completely straight, shoulders back and chin perfectly level with the floor.

The lovely flush tinting her cheeks gave away her internal agitation, however.

"What kind of proposal?" she finally asked.

A slow smile spread across Jonah's face. "It's perfect." The tempo of his voice picked up as he made his pitch. "I have been researching the ranch for Natural Shale. We have that letter"—he waved at the paper she still held—"in its entirety, of course. It's almost certainly enough to tie you up in court for a while."

LeeAnn's face blanched. "Are you threatening me?" Her voice came out as a bare whisper.

"Not at all. The opposite, actually. I'm trying to help." He leaned forward a bit—not enough to invade her personal space, but enough to convey his sincerity. "Your taxes are coming due soon." A slight wave of his hand took in the entirety of Cowbelles. "And working here isn't likely to help you pay that bill."

Her mouth dropped open, and Jonah rushed to finish before she had a chance to object. "If you get caught up in court, you'll have attorneys' fees, as well—and you will be required to provide access to any paperwork that might prove the issue one way or the other. So here's what I suggest: I will pay you to let me sort through any paperwork you might have. You'll be able to pay your taxes and avoid legal fees, and with any luck, I will learn who actually holds the drilling rights to your ranch."

Pleased with his plan—*one that could help us both, one that surely even a flaky hippie chick could appreciate*—he waited confidently for her to agree.

The flush that suffused her cheeks deepened as her eyes grew wider. When she spoke, her voice shook with suppressed rage. "You've been doing research on my ranch? On *me*? You know when my taxes are due?"

Mentioning that so specifically might have been a tactical error.

"What on God's green earth makes you think I would ever let you anywhere near my property?" Her voice grew louder as she marched toward him, glancing around, almost as if she were searching for something to use as a weapon against him. "You slimy...stalker. I don't want your filthy oil money. And I definitely don't want you digging through my gran's things. What if you find something that proves I own the rights? I can't trust you to tell me. You can take your *proposal* and shove it right—"

Every muscle in her entire sleek body tightened in an apparent effort to stop herself from saying anything else. Her bunched fists shuddered, and in a deeply controlled movement, she held the photocopied letter out toward him.

"Take this," she rasped, "and get out. Now."

He'd been wrong. She was obviously too irrational to recognize a good deal when she heard one. And she was far too wrought up to listen to any of his carefully marshaled arguments right now. Brushing away a flicker of irritation, he reminded himself to remain logical.

There's no room for emotions in negotiations.

Time to retreat and regroup.

He nodded and touched the brim of his hat. "You can keep that," he said, gesturing toward the paper in her hand. Then he moved toward the exit and stepped outside.

Lord, save me from hippies.

As the closing glass door cut off the sound of the electronic chimes, he glanced back inside.

LeeAnn stood with both arms wrapped around her torso, staring at the floor, her face a mask of misery.

Then, as he watched, she straightened up, drew in a deep breath, closed her eyes, and stretched her arms toward the ceiling, standing tall and straight, the distress on her face shifting to calm determination.

The expression seemed to pull at him, drawing him toward her. Resolutely turning away, Jonah reminded himself that the most important thing he could do was finish this job and get his promotion.

Onward and upward, man. Gotta keep moving.

No room for emotions, huh?

Then why was he suddenly so determined to find a way to work with this beautiful, angry, infuriating woman?

Chapter Four

In the dressing room at the TexZen Yoga Studio, LeeAnn stared blankly into her locker for a moment. Then she tugged out her backpack and slung it over her shoulder alongside her rolled-up mat in its carrying straps. Usually, she took a quick shower after teaching a class, but today she didn't feel up to it. In fact, when Angie had called her last night and asked her to teach two classes this morning rather than her usual one, LeeAnn had almost said no—but the combination of extra money in her paycheck and a chance to remind Angie and the other instructors that she would be a good permanent addition to their team had overshadowed her desire to decline.

Not that she had gotten much sleep, anyway.

Instead, she spent the night tossing and turning, reviewing the events of the last few days—from the moment she had seen Darrell in the diner, to the kiss, to the realization that her handsome coconspirator in the sham kiss was the same man who had been calling every week, trying to torment her into allowing his company to desecrate the land her gran had given her.

Right up to the moment he had revealed his true nature: a shifty, underhanded sneak, trying to worm his way onto the ranch so he could slip the mineral rights out from under her.

She shouldn't have been surprised.

But the juxtaposition of the two very different Jonah Hamiltons had thrown her for a loop.

On one hand, he was the smooth-talking salesman who was trying to trick her into collaborating with an evil oil company. On the other hand, he was the amazingly good fake kisser with an easy smile and a willingness to help her show up her ex.

It had all been too much to process.

Besides, some traitorous voice inside her head kept whispering things like, *that wasn't a fake kiss. That was a very real kiss.*

And now here she was, sitting on a bench in the dressing room, staring off into space thinking about Jonah Hamilton instead of tying her shoes.

What is wrong with me?

She bent over to finish the job she had so absentmindedly begun, then headed out into the studio lobby.

Wait. I really should leave Angie a note about the new student who joined my class today—she should probably be in the intermediate class, but I'll let Angie decide.

Turning down the hall that led to the main office, she paused when she heard Angie's voice floating toward her. "We're glad to have you on board."

Chairs scraped across the floor in the office, but LeeAnn felt nailed to the floor.

Surely it's just another new student.

Maybe even the one who was in the class this morning.

"Thanks so much," another voice said. "I wasn't certain I'd be able to find work in another studio so quickly."

Not a new student.

A new instructor.

Who isn't me.

Finally, her feet unglued from the floor—but as she took one huge, silent step backward, the two women stepped out of the office.

The new instructor, a tiny brunette, turned back to speak to Angie one last time. "So I'll be here tomorrow for the evening class."

The evening class? That's my class. A morning class three times a week, and an evening class every day. I've been teaching it for months.

Her eyes pricked with tears, and she blinked several times, hard.

Wait. Angie asked me to cover her class in order to interview someone else? Someone for the job she knew I wanted?

At that moment, Angie glanced up and noticed LeeAnn. Her face paled a little, but she continued speaking to the new hire.

"That sounds great," the studio owner said to the new instructor, shaking the woman's hand and nodding.

LeeAnn turned to let the smaller woman by but couldn't manage more than a nod in response to the other woman's smile and murmured greeting.

"Could I speak to you for a moment, LeeAnn?" Angie asked, gesturing into her office.

No.

"Of course." Blinking back more tears, she followed her boss into the office.

Angie took a seat behind the desk and gestured for LeeAnn to sit down, as well.

"You know we love you here," Angie said, her voice kind.

No.

LeeAnn nodded.

"You've done a wonderful job filling in while we've been shorthanded, and your work with the beginners' classes has been excellent."

But? Is there a "but" coming?

"We want you to keep teaching those classes." Angie's tone tilted up at the end of the statement, even though it wasn't a question. The studio owner clearly wasn't done speaking, but she paused as if to give LeeAnn a chance to say something. When she didn't respond, Angie continued. "But you are still at least two months away from finishing your certification."

There's the "but." And it comes with a head tilt from Angie—that's supposed to indicate sympathy, I think.

It's not working.

"Maria has been teaching for several years in some prestigious studios. We couldn't turn down her application." Angie pursed her lips a little. "You understand, right?"

"Of course." LeeAnn's voice sounded scratchy with tears. She cleared her throat. "So Maria isn't taking over my night class?"

"Not at all. We're adding an intermediate class in the evenings. Maria is taking over several of my classes so I can do more administrative work."

Well, that's something, I guess.

Not a full-time job sort of something, but at least not a "you're fired" type of something, either.

If I don't get out of here, I'm going to start crying.

Standing abruptly, LeeAnn nodded. "Sounds great. Thanks for letting me know. I've got to get over to Cowbelles. Kylie's not back until tomorrow."

"I'm glad you understand," Angie said to LeeAnn's retreating back.

But she didn't understand—not really—and she fumed about it all the way over to the gift shop.

Angie has known me for years. She knew I wanted that job, that I've been working toward it for ages now.

Once again she blinked back tears, this time as she unlocked the door to the store.

First Darrell, and now this.

She flipped the light switches with a little more force than necessary, then made her way to the stockroom to drop her gear. A glance in the mirror showed her a face splotchy with unshed tears, so she splashed water on it in the bathroom sink. She envied women who could cry prettily—Kylie, for example, got a little pink at the end of her nose when she cried. She looked cute.

Not me. She peered at the big red blotches across her cheeks and around her eyes. *And that's before the tears come.*

Usually, she would brush on a little powder and lip gloss to make up for the blotches—but today she didn't even feel like doing that much. Pushing away from the sink, she puffed out a sigh.

What a horrible week.

Her lip trembled as she once again fought back tears.

I have to get this under control.

What yoga pose would work for this kind of misery?

She squeezed her eyes closed, thinking hard.

Inversions.

Inverted asanas were good for bringing new light to old situations.

I could definitely use a new viewpoint.

Moving back into the showroom, she grabbed a T-shirt off the nearest shelf. "I'll pay for it later," she muttered to herself. Plopping it onto the cold, hard tile floor in the back corner of the room, she knelt down in front of the makeshift pad.

Pay attention to body placement.

Arms in a triangle. Protect the neck.

Head on the floor.

Knees up on the elbows.

Lift the legs with control.

Once her body was in perfect alignment, she closed her eyes and focused on her breath.

In. Out.

Relax into the pose.

Om.

The world slipped away, leaving in its wake a quiet silence, the peace that she never could find in the outside world.

So deep was she into the meditation that she almost didn't hear the electronic jingle of the door opening. The sound finally penetrated the wall of serenity she had constructed around herself, and she took a last deep breath in and blew it back out.

When she opened her eyes, she gasped, her legs wobbling in the air until she leaned them against the wall.

Squatting down in front of her was Jonah Hamilton, the tips of his cowboy boots less than six inches from her face, his own head tilted so far over that it was almost as upside down as she was.

"Hey," he said, one dimple flashing in a half smile. "How's it going?"

Well. That's certainly a new viewpoint.

• • •

When Jonah walked into the shop, it had taken him several moments to find LeeAnn—and then it took a few seconds for his brain to fully process what his eyes were seeing when he finally saw what she was doing.

Well, crazy upside-down hippie chick or no, he needed access to her land to get his promotion.

After he spoke to her, she blinked a couple of times.

"How's it going? Actually? Pretty crappy." Gently pushing off from the wall, she folded her legs down toward the floor in a controlled bend, forcing him to stand up and take a step back.

"What's up?" he asked.

Shaking her head as she grabbed a folded T-shirt from the floor, she moved toward the cash register.

She's about to put that damned counter between us again. Oh, no, you don't.

Jonah lengthened his stride to get in front of her and

stopped, holding out one arm and bracing his hand on the wall to block her from getting past him. "I've had a brilliant idea."

"Oh, yeah?" LeeAnn ducked under his outstretched arm and kept moving. "What's that?" Spinning on one heel, he followed her.

"Why don't I pay you to be my assistant?"

The way her back stiffened when she stopped made it clear that he'd hit a nerve.

But which one? And why?

If only he could read her as well as his other clients. What was it about her that kept him so off balance?

She didn't turn around when she spoke. "Assisting with what?"

"Going through all the paperwork out at your ranch. That way you will know everything that I know, as I know it." He paused, uncertain if he should bring up the issue that had set her off the day before. Then he plunged ahead anyway. "If you're my research assistant, then you won't have to worry about what's going on behind the scenes. You'll know."

Anticipation stopped his breath as he waited for her reply.

When she finally did look at him, a tiny frown line furrowed her brow. "You want to pay me to help you go through the paperwork that might allow you to drill on my land? To find a way to do the one thing I want to avoid at all costs?"

Gently. Move very carefully.

She's skittish, but she hasn't run away yet.

"It's not as crazy as it sounds," he said, keeping his voice low and soothing. "If I don't manage to track down the information they need, then Natural Shale will bring in the lawyers—the letter, along with the lack of any other information will give them enough leverage to make a claim against you. They'll force you to produce all the paperwork anyway—and then you'll either have to hire your own lawyers or accept that they'll win."

"So what you're saying is that you work for a bunch of bullies?" Her frown deepened. Again, he had to fight the urge to smooth it away, even though he knew that touching her would be the worst move he could make right now. Especially since she was finally paying attention, listening to his words rather than flying into a rage. Maybe he could get a logical response out of her after all. He had to try.

"No," he said. "What I'm saying is that there's a good chance you'll have to do this work anyway—you might as well get something out of it."

"What do you get out of it?" She turned her back again and headed toward the counter. Her tone suggested that she didn't care about his answer one way or the other, but every line of her body said otherwise.

Why does this suddenly matter more to her now than it did yesterday?

Jonah hated working without all the pertinent information.

"If they bring in the lawyers, I lose any chance at a bonus," he said. It wasn't the whole truth, but he wasn't about to tell her he had a promotion riding on this deal. And he didn't even want to admit to himself that part of the appeal of his plan was spending more time with this infuriating woman.

"What if we discover that the drilling rights belong to me after all?" She still wasn't looking at him, dammit. He needed to see her eyes.

Well, at least she can't see how much it matters to me.

Best not to examine that thought too closely, either.

"Then I'm out a little cash, that's all." He tried to put the accompanying shrug into his tone, even though she wasn't looking. It took everything he had to keep quiet after his statement, to wait for her to make up her mind.

"And if we find evidence that allows your company to drill?" Her voice was so low that he almost couldn't hear it.

The urge to comfort her swept through him, and taking a step forward, he reached out as if to place his hand on her shoulder.

What the hell am I doing?

Be businesslike. Act like a professional, dumbass. "Then you would have to accept that. But as the landowner, you would still have certain rights that will help you protect your ranch. If it comes to it, there are people who can help with that element."

She's going to say no. He knew it with the kind of certainty that had served him through hundreds of negotiations, and he began marshaling further arguments to try to convince her.

After a long, silent moment, she nodded.

"Okay," she said.

Closing his mouth on the words he was about to say, he stared at her in disbelief. He should have felt relief. Instead, the defeat echoing through her voice felt like a punch to the stomach.

What had he just done?

Chapter Five

What did I just do?

Saying that single word—*okay*—made her head spin and her stomach clench, as if by merely agreeing to examine the documents, she had betrayed her gran, the ranch...her entire world.

But at least this way she would be able to pay the taxes.

Another year without taking out a mortgage. The ranch was hers, free and clear—exactly as she had promised Gran.

So why did she feel so awful?

"What's next?" she finally asked, once again turning to face Jonah Hamilton. Looking at him sent irrational shivers up her spine, made her want to say yes to anything he suggested. She had kept her back to him through most of the discussion, knowing that if she faced him, she'd be lost.

But now?

Time to put on my big-girl panties.

I don't have many other options, and this will allow me

to pay the taxes. So I need to accept it. I've made a deal with this devil.

An amazingly handsome devil.

"I thought maybe we could set up a time to talk later today. When do you get off work?" Jonah's smile nearly blinded her. Although she understood why he would want to beat the lawyers to the punch by finding any paperwork that might exist, she had no idea why he trusted her to play fair, or how he thought paying her would benefit him if the precious paperwork he wanted didn't exist.

"Are you usually a gambler?" she asked, rather than answering his question.

Those dimples flashed into existence again. "Only when the stakes are right," he said.

What does that mean?

Rather than follow that line of thought, LeeAnn said, "I want to talk about this a little more, if it's okay with you." When he nodded, she continued. "I have a yoga class tonight. We can meet after—eight thirty? There's a coffee shop on Main and Exchange. But talking isn't going to do any good. Gran left everything to me. You'll see." The electronic bell over the door jingled, and LeeAnn turned toward it.

"Maybe so," Jonah said. "But it's my job to verify that." He tipped his hat as he passed the woman who had entered the store, then, turning back to LeeAnn as he pushed open the door, grinned and said, "And now it's your job, too."

• • •

Jonah was waiting outside the coffee shop when she arrived. An entire day of trying to come up with alternatives to his plan had left her exhausted and distracted, and the way his figure drew her eyes didn't help her concentration.

The driver of the bright red pickup coming out of the parking lot wasn't paying any more attention than LeeAnn was as she stepped onto the asphalt entrance that crossed the sidewalk. She didn't even notice the vehicle until Jonah reached out and grabbed her arm, pulling her up against him.

The squeal of brakes was almost instantly replaced by the revving of the truck's engine, and the truck peeled out of the lot, the driver scowling at LeeAnn and Jonah as he drove past.

"Are you okay?" Jonah asked, his grip tight on her upper arms.

Still working to catch her breath, LeeAnn blinked up at him. Crushed against him, she could feel every inch of him—and of the reaction her closeness was eliciting. Her nipples tightened in response. The heat of his body pressed up against her seemed to steal her voice, and she cast around frantically for something to say.

Something besides, "Oh, my, what big arms you have."
And other…things.

In that context, a glance at the retreating pickup almost made her giggle. "I hate those," she finally said, pointing at the trailer hitch of the truck. Jonah glanced over his shoulder to follow her gesture.

"Trucks that try to run you over? I don't blame you." He settled her on her feet and brushed his hands up and down her arms, his gaze searching as if to reassure himself that she was really okay. With a nod, Jonah opened the door to the coffee shop and ushered her inside.

She snorted, her voice still shaky. "Those, too. But no. I meant the stupid plastic testicles hanging off the back end."

The landman gestured for her to choose a seat. "So is it the testicles themselves that you object to, or the fact that they're plastic?"

She appreciated his willingness to ignore her adrenaline-induced shakiness.

Definitely adrenaline. Not other…things.

"I think they're tacky," she said. She stared up at the chalkboard menu above the counter, then turned to Jonah. "I'll take a chai soy latte, please."

His dimples flashed for a bare second, and he nodded.

Wishing she could read his mind—what was he grinning about?—she made her way back to one of the tiny bistro tables.

Business. This is a business meeting.

No matter how her body reacted to him.

Deep breath. Om.

• • •

Jonah watched with interest as LeeAnn stood up on the tips of her toes and came back down next to the small table and chair by a window. He half expected her to stand on her head before she sat down. Instead, she simply slid into the seat and settled her shoulders in a straight-backed stance.

It was that nervous habit yoga again—at least this time she hadn't moved into the full crane-like pose.

Besides, she almost got run down. Give her a minute to get over it.

He was having to work to ignore the fact that the whole

incident made him want to kill the idiot in the truck, then wrap LeeAnn in his arms to make sure no one ever hurt her again.

Minutes later, he was seated across from her. He took a sip of his plain black coffee and watched her breathe in the steam from her chai, waiting for her to break the silence.

"If I'm really going to work for you, I need more information," she said. "Let's start over from the beginning. Explain to me again what it is, exactly, that you do." LeeAnn leaned back in the coffee shop booth, her blond hair bright against the red vinyl.

Jonah matched her casual posture, a technique he had learned years ago that helped create trust. "I'm a landman. Basically, I'm something of a cross between a lawyer and a real estate agent for mineral rights. I track down titles, sort through wills, and work to find out who owns the right to mine or drill on any given piece of land. Once that's settled, I arrange for right-of-way and drilling leases."

"And you're particularly interested in my ranch because…?"

Her tone had turned suspicious again, so Jonah worked to keep his as businesslike as possible. "A recent geological survey indicated that there's a good chance we'll find a natural gas reservoir. I've been contracted to find the mineral rights to your land and the land surrounding your ranch."

"Why not drill on someone else's land, then?" She took a sip of her drink. "Couldn't you get to the gas that way?"

He nodded. "You're right. All we really need is to tap into the reservoir—under your land or your neighbor's really doesn't matter. Once we sink a producing well, it will draw from the entire reservoir. But we haven't been able to track down the Abrams' mineral rights, either, and the Stephensons, who have clear mineral rights to their land, have refused to allow us to drill on their ranch. So for the moment, that leaves you."

"Okay. So you track down the rights. And then?" She watched him carefully.

"Then I start working out an offer to lease the mineral rights, and we drill."

"If the offer is accepted." Picking up a napkin, she began tearing off tiny pieces and rolling them between her forefinger and thumb.

"Right." He took a drink of his own coffee.

"So what do you need from me?"

"The easiest thing would be if you have the paperwork proving you own the mineral rights—or proving that they went to someone else."

"I have no idea where to even start looking." She didn't look up from the tiny pile of napkin balls she was creating.

"You inherited the house and land from your grandmother, right? Did she have any legal papers?" Jonah had to fight the urge to reach out and still her hands.

"I don't know where that kind of paperwork might be," she said. She paused for a moment, staring at him through narrowed eyes. "If it's anywhere at all."

He shrugged. "I'll take my chances, then. We should probably start by going through all her papers to see if we can find anything that might help trace the rights."

LeeAnn's harsh bark of laughter startled him. "I don't think you know what you're asking. Gran was a bit of a pack rat, to put it mildly. Honestly? She could have ended up on that *Hoarders* television show. She had a habit of filling up an outbuilding then slapping a padlock on it and leaving it. I've been working on sorting through them, but I've barely gotten started."

He shook his head. "Come on. It can't be that bad. How many outbuildings are there?"

"Six. Plus the old stables." Sweeping the pile of shredded napkin balls off the table and into her hand, she dumped them into her empty cup.

"And all of them are full? Of what?"

Rather than answering his question, she slid out of the booth and stood up.

"I think it might be better if you saw for yourself. I'm not sure it will be worth your time, but you're welcome to come over Saturday and check it out." She grinned at him, and the smile went straight through his chest. "You have no idea what you're getting into, but sure, be my guest."

"Why not tomorrow?" he asked.

"My boss from Cowbelles gets back tomorrow," she replied, swinging her backpack over her shoulder. "I won't have time."

"Okay," he said, and stood up. He plucked his hat off the table and settled it on his head. "What time should I be there on Saturday?"

"If you're serious about going through anything, you'll need all day. Let's start in the morning. Eight?"

"I'll be there." He watched her as she slipped out of the coffee shop, her step light, her hips swaying in a way he found utterly hypnotic.

That conversation had gone about as well as he could have hoped—really, he reminded himself, it was no surprise that LeeAnn so vehemently opposed the idea of drilling on her land, given her job as a yoga instructor. Those types tended to despise everything about what he did.

But that didn't mean she couldn't like *him*, right?

He sighed, irritated with his own response to the woman.

As much as he'd liked his plan to hire her as his assistant when he came up with it, he was beginning to think that perhaps he wasn't thinking logically about her at all.

The sooner he finished this job and moved into his new position, the better off he would be.

So why was he looking forward to Saturday so much?

Chapter Six

LeeAnn was only one long talk away from figuring all this out.

Because that's what best friends were for, right? She had been ecstatic the night before when she checked her phone messages and discovered that Kylie had gotten home a day early. She'd called the store owner back after she had washed off the dust from crawling through the attic to pull out the single box of paperwork she knew existed, and they had made a date to meet up at Azteca for dinner—LeeAnn had suggested lunch, but Kylie had wanted the day to unpack and get settled at home.

Now they were sitting at a back table, and LeeAnn had begun telling Kylie everything.

Well, almost everything. She hadn't exactly detailed how…unsettled…being around Jonah made her feel.

But she had given all of the pertinent facts.

How I feel isn't significant to the story.

"Wait. You fell down?" Kylie leaned over the table between them, her mouth hanging slightly open. "You? You're the most graceful person I know."

"Oh, it gets worse." LeeAnn dropped her purse into the unoccupied chair beside her. "Then I kissed him."

Kylie leaned back in her seat. "Okay. Back up. Start at the beginning. You walked into the new diner and saw Darrell."

LeeAnn nodded and began talking. By the time she had finished, Kylie had both hands over her mouth in an attempt to stifle her laughter.

"Oh, sweetie," Kylie said. "And now you're going to work for him? That's…I don't even know what that is."

"It's screwed up, is what it is." Rubbing her eyes with her knuckles, LeeAnn shook her head. "I cannot believe my life."

Kylie ripped open a pink packet of sweetener and dumped it into her tea. Then she tilted her head and gazed at her friend for a long moment. LeeAnn waited for her to say something.

Anything.

But preferably something insightful.

Maybe even inspirational.

"So," Kylie finally asked, "which Superman?"

"What?" It felt for a moment like the room had tilted—the question was so unexpected that LeeAnn had to shake her head to try to make sense of it. "What do you mean, which Superman?"

"I mean, are we talking the nineteen fifties television Superman? Because honestly?" Kylie pursed her lips and shook her head. "Not so hotso."

"No. Not that one." With a nod of thanks to the waitress who had set down their drinks, LeeAnn pulled a menu out of the stack on the table, and, taking a sip of her own, unsweetened tea, she narrowed her eyes at her friend. "You know what I mean. Dark hair, blue eyes. Pretty face."

"So maybe Christopher Reeve's Superman?" Kylie squeezed a lemon into the drink with one hand and used the other to stir with her straw. "He was pretty."

LeeAnn opened her menu and stared down at it, but she couldn't focus enough to even read the options. "Why are we having this conversation?"

"Oh, I'm just getting started. There's Tom Welling's *Smallville* Superman." LeeAnn's friend nibbled thoughtfully on her bottom lip. "Too young in the early seasons, but by the end of the series? He'd probably do."

LeeAnn sighed and shook her head. "You're insane. You realize that, right?"

"Then there was that guy from *Lois & Clark* in the nineties. He was totally hot." She began ticking them off on her fingers. "The *Superman Returns* guy? Gorgeous. But really, I hope it's not him, because that's a stupid movie. Superman is *not* a baby daddy."

"I hope not," LeeAnn muttered.

Flashing a grin at her friend, Kylie kept counting. "There was a Prius ad, but I'm not sure that counts. And then there's Henry Cavill." She fanned herself as she took a sip of tea. "He'd be my choice."

"How do you know all of this? I don't think I could name even one Superman actor," LeeAnn said.

"Are you kidding? I've been on the road with my musician boyfriend for weeks. I'm glad he has Netflix in the tour bus."

"Seriously? Calling that behemoth a bus is like calling the Ritz a motel. Of course Cole's bus has Netflix. Anyway, surely you could think of much better things to do than watch old Superman shows."

A pink blush crawled across Kylie's cheeks. "I got bored watching the rehearsals all the time."

"Yeah. Rehearsals. That's what I was talking about," LeeAnn said, her tone turning dry. "So, really, you hid in the tour bus the whole time? Weren't you checking out new cities, finding all the local hot spots?"

"I wasn't hiding," Kylie protested. "I did all that stuff, too. Sort of."

"Admit it," LeeAnn said. "You barely set foot out of the bus unless Cole was with you. You spent all that time watching television and waiting for him to get done rehearsing so he could go out with you."

"We have gotten off topic." Kylie finally flipped open her own menu. "We are discussing your love life, not mine."

LeeAnn snorted. "My love life is nonexistent, unless you count being dumped on my ass, and then falling on my ass, as a love life."

"You forgot kissing Superman," Kylie teased. "Then going to work for him."

"I've lost my mind, haven't I?" LeeAnn moaned, covering her eyes with her hands.

"You know you can come to work full-time with me." Kylie's tone changed from teasing to earnest, and she stretched one hand out, placing it on the table in front of her friend. "You don't have to take the job with this guy if you don't want to. You're not stuck having to take his offer, even if stupid TexZen doesn't realize how much they need you."

"Thanks," LeeAnn said, placing her own hand atop Kylie's. "I really do appreciate it. But Cowbelles can't support both of us yet. Don't forget, I've been running the store for the last three weeks—I've seen the numbers."

"We can make it work," Kylie said.

"No." LeeAnn shook her head. "This is really the best option. I'll go back to working weekends and whatever other times you need me. Anyway, if the mineral rights don't belong to me, I need to know about it."

"If they do belong to you?" Kylie asked. "What then?"

"If they do, then I will have legal proof and can send the Natural Shale lawyers packing when they show up." She gave a determined nod.

"And Superman? Will you send him packing, too?" LeeAnn didn't like the intent stare her friend gave her as she asked the question.

"Yeah," she said. "Him, too." She tried to put conviction into her tone, but it came out sounding more tentative than she had intended.

Why did saying it send a pain through her stomach?

"Okay, then," Kylie said. "Now that I'm back, you don't have to come in for a few weeks—unless you need the cash. But it sounds like he's paying you enough that it won't be a problem."

LeeAnn made a small noise of agreement, but she was still thinking about sending Jonah away. Dropping her hands into her lap, she stared down at them, her fingers twisting around each other.

She wanted to get rid of him. Getting rid of Jonah Hamilton was high on the top of her to-do list.

Then why did the thought of it make her anxious enough to want to start doing back bends in the middle of the restaurant?

When she glanced up, she realized that Kylie was still staring at her—and had been for quite some time.

"Well, then," her best friend said, picking up her menu and nodding to herself. "I'm guessing he's Henry Cavill hot."

"So, anything else exciting happen while I was gone?" Kylie asked after dinner as they strolled down the sidewalk toward Cowbelles.

LeeAnn shrugged. "I tried to quit cursing again."

With a laugh, her friend looped her arm through Lee-Ann's and hugged it to her side. "And how did that go?"

"Not too well," LeeAnn admitted.

"I figured as much." Kylie laughed again. "I know you really want to be the amazing yogi woman, all serene and calm. But you might as well accept that fact that at best, you'll be something of a redneck yogi."

"I am not a redneck," LeeAnn protested.

"Not really," Kylie said, "but you're a Texan. You own a ranch and a horse. And you can't quit cursing, no matter how hard you try. In fact, you kind of curse like a sailor."

"Aw, hell," LeeAnn said in her best Texas drawl, fighting a grin. "I am a redneck yogi, aren't I?"

The two women were half bent over with laughter as they passed the parking lot that backed up to the Wagon Wheel Diner. "Oh my God," LeeAnn said, dragging them to a halt, staring over Kylie's back. "I can't believe he did that."

"Can't believe who did what?" Kylie pulled away and glanced around nervously.

LeeAnn waved her hand wildly in the direction of the parking lot. "That smart-ass put testicles on his truck."

"What are you talking about?" Kylie asked.

LeeAnn took her friend by the shoulders and spun her around to face the parking lot, then pointed at the back of the truck. "See? Right there. Those Truck Nutz hanging off that green pickup?"

Kylie nodded. "Okay, I see them."

"Last night," LeeAnn said, "I told Jonah that I hated those things. So he went out and got some, just to screw with me."

Kylie's mouth opened once or twice before she finally replied. "Are you sure?"

"They're right there." LeeAnn's voice rose in indignation. "Look at them."

"I mean, are you sure that's Jonah's truck?" Pressing her lips together, the store owner squinted a bit at her friend.

"Of course I'm sure. How many old green pickups do you see around here?" Spinning in a complete circle, Lee-Ann indicated the whole parking lot.

Kylie made a noncommittal noise.

"I can't let him get away with it." A decisive nod punctuated the statement.

"Get away with what?" Kylie asked. "It's his truck. He can do whatever he wants to with it."

"Not this time. Come on." LeeAnn grabbed her friend's hand and began tugging her toward the sidewalk.

Kylie planted her feet on the asphalt. "Where are we going?"

"To the hardware store." With one final, sharp tug, Lee-Ann made sure both women were headed out of the parking lot. "They're open until nine, I think."

Kylie's last comment sounded more resigned than actively glum. "This isn't going to end well, is it?"

Chapter Seven

Fifteen minutes later, armed with a brand-new pair of gardening shears, the two women stood in the alley behind the diner.

LeeAnn crouched down low and peered around the corner. Catching a glimpse of movement near the green pickup, she ducked back behind the brick wall again.

"I really think this is a bad idea," Kylie hissed from behind her.

"No, it's not," LeeAnn said, trying to keep her voice to a whisper. "Those things are offensive. Seriously, what man in his right mind hangs plastic testicles off the trailer hitch of his truck?" She didn't give Kylie a chance to respond before continuing. "I'll tell you who. A rude, sexist, obnoxious jerk whose truck takes the place of any real masculinity he might have. That's who." By the time she finished her mini rant, her voice had risen to something below a shout.

Kylie slapped at her back. "Would you shut up, please?

If you're really going to do this, just go, already."

Nodding, LeeAnn hefted the garden shears in one hand. "I still say we should have tried to find some real bolt cutters."

"I think those might be illegal," her friend said.

"And I think that Truck Nutz ought to be outlawed, too." Standing up straight, LeeAnn put her back against the wall. This time, there was no movement when she looked out at the truck. "Okay," she said. "You come with me and keep an eye out."

The two of them scuttled out from behind the building and into the parking lot, dashing from car to car to avoid the yellow pools of light under the lampposts dotting the pavement.

When they reached the pickup, LeeAnn crouched down and grabbed Kylie's hand, dragging the shop owner down beside her. "Look at these," she hissed, gesturing at the dangling ornament. "They're tacky and disgusting."

"I've changed my mind," Kylie said. "I don't want to do this. I think castrating someone else's truck might be even more illegal than carrying bolt cutters."

"You know he thinks they make him manlier." LeeAnn centered the shears on the coated wire that attached the offending decoration to the hitch.

"And Cole will never let me hear the end of it if we get caught." Kylie began chewing on her bottom lip—a nervous habit she'd had for as long as LeeAnn had known her.

"He's. Better. Off. Without. Them." Tiny grunts punctuated each word as LeeAnn began applying pressure to the shears, working to force them through the wire.

"We'll end up in the tabloids again." Clasping her hands together, Kylie rocked back and forth slightly. "I can see the headlines: *Cole Grayson's Girlfriend Arrested for Emasculating a Truck*."

"There," LeeAnn said triumphantly. "One wire down, one to go."

"That's it. I'm going to jail," Kylie whispered.

With a slight *thunk*, the shears severed the second wire, and the flesh-colored object fell into LeeAnn's waiting palm. "Gross," she said.

"What are you going to do with them?" her friend asked.

"Hang them over my door, maybe? No, wait. I know—let's use them to replace the bell at Cowbelles." She snickered, bouncing the plastic testicles in her hand. "We can change the name to Cowballs."

"Yeah, right. Great. Let's get out of here." Kylie stood up, then froze in place as headlights swept across her face. "Someone else is here," she hissed.

"Of course they are. It's a parking lot. Let's go." LeeAnn stood up, tugging at her friend's sleeve as she began to turn around.

"LeeAnn? Is that you?"

She jumped and squeaked a little at the sound of the deep voice from behind her. She shoved the truck nuts behind her back as she turned to face Jonah. "You startled me."

"I see that." A tiny frown indented his forehead. "What's up?"

"We're…headed home from dinner." LeeAnn could tell her voice was still too high, but she couldn't seem to bring it back down.

"Are you two okay?" The suspicious look on his face carried over to his tone.

"Oh, nothing," Kylie sang out, sounding completely guilty.

"What?" Jonah asked, blinking in confusion.

"We're not doing anything." Kylie shook her head emphatically, and LeeAnn frowned, wishing she had the power to make her friend shut up—but she had to settle for shooting a quelling look at her.

"We're fine," LeeAnn replied, working to sound normal. "How are you?"

Cheerful but normal—that's the plan.

"I'm doing well," he replied, his own voice anything but normal.

He's already suspicious. I need to make sure he doesn't see what we've done to his truck. Or what's in my hand.

"So," she said, working to buy time. "You headed out?" A quick glance told her it would take only a step or two to stand between Jonah and the evidence of his mutilated Truck Nutz. As Jonah shifted on his feet, LeeAnn turned to keep him from viewing what was in her hand. *Sidestep one… two…and now he can't see the hitch.*

"Nope," Jonah replied. "Just got here."

So why is he back out in the parking lot? "Did you leave something in your truck?" she asked.

Lean back against the tailgate. Act casual.

LeeAnn's heart raced.

Now that he's seen us out here, he'll know we were the ones who castrated his truck. How can I reattach these without him seeing?

• • •

LeeAnn was practically two-stepping back and forth in front of Jonah, while her friend—Kylie, he remembered, the one who owned the shop where LeeAnn worked part-time — twisted her hands and chewed on her bottom lip.

They're definitely nervous. What the hell are these two up to?

"Did you leave something in your truck?" Instead of turning this time, LeeAnn took a big, sliding step sideways until she stood with her back against the tailgate. Watching him carefully, she leaned back against it, trying to act casual. It didn't work. With her arm twisted up behind her back to hide what she had in her hand, she looked more uncomfortable than anything.

"No," he said, frowning a little and waving toward the diner. "I was planning to get something to eat."

"Oh, okay," LeeAnn said breathlessly.

But her friend tilted her head and narrowed her eyes at him. "You just got here?" she asked.

Jonah nodded. "I saw you over here when I pulled in, so I thought I'd come say hi."

Both women went completely still, like animals in the wild when something startled them.

What did I say?

Slowly, Kylie unclasped her hands and raised them to cover her mouth. Then she let out a string of curses that would have put his biggest, strongest, hardest-living, toughest-talking cowboy friends to shame.

LeeAnn didn't curse. In fact, she didn't say anything — but her face went completely white.

"Why don't you two go ahead and tell me what's going on," he said. "Maybe I can help."

Silently, LeeAnn pulled her hand from behind her back and held it out toward him, a pair of plastic bull testicles hanging from the wires gripped in her closed fist.

He paused for a moment, taking in the sight of the

beautiful yoga instructor in a pair of blue jeans and a tight T-shirt that outlined every curve, dangling toy balls at him.

He couldn't decide if it was hot, or terrifying.

Anyway, why was she showing him giant plastic nuts?

When she stepped away from the rear of the Ford—the green, fifties-era Ford—it all clicked.

A slow grin spread across his face, then he erupted in a snort of laughter.

"Shut up," Kylie hissed, glancing around the parking lot. "You're going to get us arrested."

LeeAnn's face turned a bright shade of pink. "This isn't your truck, is it?"

"No," Jonah managed to get out, in between guffaws. "It's not."

She stared at the balls in her hand. "We're going to have to figure out how to reattach these."

Kylie shook her head. "I think that truck castration might be permanent," she said mournfully. Then a tiny snicker escaped her. LeeAnn glared at her friend for a moment—and suddenly the two women were leaning on one another, howling with laughter.

"Oh, dear," LeeAnn said, waving the balls back and forth. "I don't know what to do about these."

"I think I can help you out," Jonah said. "I'll be right back."

Jogging back to his truck, he opened the toolbox in the back and rummaged around, coming up with a length of baling wire and a pair of pliers.

"Give them to me," he said as he got back to the two women. LeeAnn handed over the testicles and crouched down next to him as he worked to reattach them to the trailer hitch. "Keep an eye out?" he said to Kylie, who nodded and stared around the parking lot, her arms crossed over her chest.

"I can't believe we're putting these back on," LeeAnn said.

"I can't believe you thought they were mine." Suppressed laughter threaded through his voice. He pushed his Stetson back on his head to see better, then twisted the wire up through the hitch connection.

"Why wouldn't I? It's not like there are that many trucks like yours around." She jerked her chin up toward the truck above them. As she leaned back in to watch him, her shoulder brushed against his, sending a tiny electric shock through his entire body.

Pay attention, Hamilton.

Right. Pay attention. To the testicles in my hand.

Great.

"Are you kidding? This is nothing like my truck." With a final twist, he cut the wire and pulled on the decoration to make sure it was securely attached. Standing, he tucked the pliers into a back pocket of his Levi's. "This is a Ford. Probably a 1958 or so. Look at that clunky hood, the square grill. No. *My* truck is a 1956 Chevy—chrome bumpers, small-block V-8 engine. They're nothing at all alike."

"They're *exactly* alike," LeeAnn protested, moving in one fluid motion to stand up. "Old green pickups."

Resettling his hat, Jonah shook his head, a small smile playing around his lips. "I'm disappointed, Ms. Walker. I'd expect a Texas girl to know a little more about trucks."

But as soon as he said her name, LeeAnn's own smile faded. Reaching out to grab Kylie's arm, she tugged her friend back toward the gift store. "Thank you," she said to Jonah, her tone suddenly formal. "I appreciate your help."

Kylie glanced back and forth between the two. "Yes," she said. "Thanks. We really do appreciate it." With a little wave, she turned to catch up with LeeAnn, who had spun around and started marching toward Cowbelles.

Jonah watched LeeAnn walk away, her back stiff and straight.

What just happened?

"That was sort of rude," Kylie said, after catching up with LeeAnn. "He did help us out—even knowing that you meant to castrate *his* truck. That was really nice of him."

"I know," LeeAnn replied. How could she explain to Kylie that the sound of his voice as he called her "Ms. Walker" had suddenly reminded her of all the times he had called her on the phone, attempting to get her to discuss allowing his company to drill on her ranch?

She could barely explain her reaction to herself.

She felt like she was on a seesaw, riding back and forth between thinking of Jonah Hamilton as the smooth-talking businessman out to screw her out of her mineral rights... and as the cowboy who pulled her out of the way of oncoming trucks and fixed her screwed-up attempt at some semi-political statement about Truck Nutz.

And who kisses like he means it…even when he doesn't.

The two women walked in silence for a moment until, with a grin, Kylie leaned over to bump against her friend with her shoulder. "*Definitely* Henry Cavill hot."

LeeAnn laughed. "Okay, okay. I have to work with him tomorrow," she said. "I can be polite then."

Chapter Eight

The next morning, LeeAnn woke early and took her yoga mat outside to the top of the hill behind her house. Out in the farthest field, bluebonnets were beginning to bloom, creating a gorgeous sea of blue and green. Closer in, the grass of an enclosure had been grazed down by her horse, Blackie, and she reminded herself that she needed to make sure none of the flowers were blooming in any of the pastures where he might eat—bluebonnets could be deadly to horses. She still had the battered copy of *Guide to Texas Plants Poisonous to Animals* the county agent had given her grandmother years ago, and over the years she had grown to enjoy weeding the pastures, especially in spring. It made her feel like she was doing something important.

She spread her mat out on the dew-damp grass and breathed in deeply. In the distance, she heard a few birds chirp, then the harsher caw of the grackles that nested in the big live oak tree that shaded the western side of the house.

Sami always said she hated the quiet out here, but it wasn't ever really quiet. Not with the sounds of the animals and insects, the wind through the tree leaves. The sky directly overhead was a bright blue, but she could see clouds gathering in the distance. Spring was by far her favorite season, in part because of the frequent thunderstorms that crashed through North Central Texas. She loved curling up in her living room with a cup of tea, watching the lightning flash.

Not that she would be able to enjoy the storm through a window today. Instead, she would be digging through the piles of stuff in one of the barns, if Jonah Hamilton had his way.

Don't overreact. Calm.

Breathe.

Stretching her arms above her, she began moving through the sun salutation asanas—the postures and stretches with which she began every day. As ever, her mind wandered, though she tried to focus on her breathing.

Jonah has no idea what he is getting himself into.

Was it wrong for her to feel a little gleeful at the thought of his reaction when he saw the outbuildings? Where should they start? Some of the buildings had been locked up for as long as LeeAnn could remember, the items stashed away well before she was born. Maybe the old stables? It was the last building Gran had closed off. She could remember a time when the ranch still had more than one horse, when all the stables were in use on a regular basis. If Gran had done anything with the mineral rights in the years before she died, the paperwork would probably be in there. It certainly hadn't been in the box she'd pulled down from the attic. That had been schoolwork from LeeAnn's childhood—stuff she hadn't even known Gran had saved.

Then again, Jonah had said that the mineral rights could have been split off from the main title years ago. If that was the case, the paperwork might very well be in one of the other buildings.

She hadn't ever done more than take a peek in a couple of them since she had inherited the ranch, preferring instead to start clearing out the rambling farmhouse—Gran's hoarding habits hadn't been limited to the outbuildings, so it had taken quite a while to comb through what had been locked away in closets and extra bedrooms.

The activity had helped her move through her grief after Gran's death.

Most of it had been junk, but there had been some lovely furniture that only needed refinishing to make it useful again, and she had run across a few pieces of beautiful costume jewelry. She had refinished the furniture herself and used it to redecorate the farmhouse. The jewelry she had given to Sami, who had the most amazing ability to wear vintage clothing and make it look chic—on LeeAnn, it looked old. She'd passed Gran's wedding china to Sami's sister, Beverly, who was most likely to use it.

But there hadn't been any legal paperwork in the main part of the house.

And other than that single box, she hadn't even gotten to the attic yet.

Oh, yeah. Jonah is going to be utterly horrified.

Maybe he'll even forget about the Truck Nutz incident.

Ignoring the blush that the memory brought to her face, she finished her sun salutation and went inside to brew a cup of tea.

This could turn out to be fun.

At least, that's what she would tell herself.

Om...

• • •

When Jonah pulled his truck into the caliche-paved driveway that led up to the old farmhouse, LeeAnn stood up from where she had been seated in one of two white wicker rocking chairs on the broad front porch.

Placing a teacup on the side table, she moved down to the bottom of the steps to greet him.

"Hi," he said, tilting his head toward her. "You ready for this?"

The glare of the rising sun behind her hid her face in shadows, so he couldn't see her exact expression. Nonetheless, he focused on the shadows of her face rather than the outline of her body, trim and muscled in yoga pants and a matching tight shirt.

"I guess," she said, her tone dubious. "I'll go change and meet you back out here."

A half step to the left brought her face into the light as she began to move back to the house. She paused, staring at him thoughtfully for a moment, then jerked her chin toward the closest outbuilding. "Feel free to start looking around." Without waiting for a reply, she headed into the house.

With a shrug, Jonah followed her direction toward a medium-sized barn. The door swung open when he pushed it. The space was much cleaner than LeeAnn had given him to expect.

Maybe this search won't take long, after all.

Then he would move on to senior landman. More responsibility, more pay, more security.

He wouldn't have to spend very much time trying to work with LeeAnn Walker.

Why did that thought make him uncomfortable? Pushing it aside, he prowled through the quiet room.

A covered saddle hung on a stand outside one of the stalls. Lifting the treated canvas, Jonah ran his hand across the well-worn leather. It was also well cared for—the saddle oil scented the entire barn, underlying the persistent smell of hay and horse. Next to the stand stood a closed box made of heavy-duty plastic, and at the back of the room was a free-standing metal storage unit. Tack closets like that weren't exactly cheap, Jonah knew.

Pulling the door open to let in more light, he checked out the rest of the stable. Only one stall seemed to be in use, though no horse currently occupied it. He unlatched the half door and swung it open, curiosity overcoming the knowledge that he certainly wasn't going to find any legal papers in the otherwise empty stall.

Once inside, he kicked aside clean hay. The wooden floor of the stall was covered with a rubberized mat—fairly new, by the look of it—and the hay had been recently placed, given the lack of any mold or mildew.

So there was—or recently had been—a horse, and like the saddle and tack, it was well taken care of.

He was beginning to see where the money went. Not toward making sure the outer perimeter fence was up or the various storage buildings were repaired, but maybe toward taking care of the things that mattered most to LeeAnn— her horse, her riding gear, and her barn, for example?

Kicking the hay back into place over the mat, Jonah stepped out of the stall and relatched the door.

He glanced around again. Unless LeeAnn's grandmother had used the hayloft as a storage space, they weren't likely to find any paperwork anywhere in here. There was an old tractor off to one side, parts scattered on the floor around it, but he didn't see how that could help him.

Still, he was drawn to it.

"I haven't been able to get it running since Gran died," LeeAnn said from behind him. "Haven't been able to sell it, either. I might not even be able to give it away, for that matter, but I haven't actually tried that yet."

Jonah didn't turn around. "My grandfather had a tractor like this one—an old-model John Deere from the fifties. The damn thing broke down all the time." He laughed softly. "I spent a lot of my childhood working on getting it running again. We worked on all types of engines together." Gently setting down the carburetor he had picked up, he faced Lee-Ann and gestured out the barn door toward his Chevy. "If it weren't for him, I wouldn't be able to keep Betty running."

"You named your truck Betty?" LeeAnn shook her head, but she was smiling.

"I heard it on some television show once." He shrugged. "I liked it."

"You seen Blackie yet?" she asked.

"That the horse?" He shook his head. "Not yet."

"Come on, then. I need to say hello before we get started. It's something of a ritual for us." She led him out of the barn, carefully latching the door behind them. "It's a bit of a hike," she warned. "I was only able to keep two pastures for him, so I chose the two best. But they aren't the two closest to the house."

More evidence that she cares more for the animal than herself?

This didn't exactly fit into his image of her as part of the hippie crowd.

"I'm up for a walk," he said, following her as she made her way down a dirt path worn into the scrubby Texas flora.

Out in the full sunlight, the sight of LeeAnn walking in front of him almost stopped him in his tracks. It wasn't like she hadn't worn formfitting clothes around him before. Her yoga gear left little about her long, lean body to the imagination. But something about the sight of her in faded denim jeans and an old gray T-shirt with "Fort Worth Stockyards" emblazoned across the back hit him right in the chest, taking his breath away. Strands of her blond hair escaped her ponytail and fluttered around her face under a straw cowboy hat with a pink bandanna replacing the hatband. And her boots were scuffed and worn—not the stylish, rhinestone-studded pink footwear he'd seen her wear when working at Cowbelles, but real work boots in plain brown leather.

The boots matched the gear in the barn. Used, but cared for.

As he looked around, he realized that the land fit that pattern, too. This was no longer a working ranch, and the lack of money was evident—hell, it was all he'd seen the first time he'd surveyed the place.

On closer inspection, though, he could see the care put into what maintenance had been done.

Not much money, but what there was had been spent well. The fence next to the horse barn showed evidence of recent patching, the newer wood showing up as a lighter color. The house hadn't been painted recently enough for his taste—it was beginning to peel—but the rain gutters were clear of debris, and the porch had been recently swept.

She hadn't exaggerated about the distance from the house—by the time they reached the small corral right outside two large fenced pastures, he couldn't see the road any longer. The ranch stood right at the edge of the Texas Hill Country, so there was just enough roll to the land to obscure any straight line of sight.

The fencing around the corral was wooden and carefully tended—no peeling paint here. The larger pastures were surrounded with wire fencing interspersed with tall wooden fence posts, and these fences were also in much better shape than the barbed-wire ones that edged that outer perimeter of the ranch.

LeeAnn skirted the smaller enclosure, coming up to lean on the nearest post by one of the pastures. Putting her fingers to her lips, she let out a piercing whistle. A rustling erupted in a small copse of trees against the eastern fence about a third of the way down pasture, and a large black gelding emerged from the spring foliage, nickering as he cantered toward them. When he reached the fence, he stopped, shook out his mane, and stretched his head out over the fence beside LeeAnn with a decided nod.

"Show-off," she murmured. Wrapping her arms around the graceful arch of his neck, LeeAnn greeted the horse. "Hey, baby," she said, grinning. "You have a good morning? Yeah? Me, too." She murmured a few other inanities, then stroked his ears as he snuffled around her hands. Laughing, she reached into her pocket and pulled out a few sugar cubes. "Looking for these?" The horse's lips flared as he delicately picked them off her outstretched palm.

Watching her interact with the animal, Jonah couldn't help but smile.

This is definitely where all her care goes.

"Want to meet him?" she finally asked, turning to Jonah.

"Sure," Jonah said.

LeeAnn's mouth quirked up in an impish grin. "I was asking the horse."

A bark of laughter escaped Jonah, and he replied, "Well, then, let me know what he says."

She bent her head back to the gelding, her blond ponytail swinging around and shining bright against the black of the horse's mane. "Yeah, he's okay with it," she finally said, her gray eyes sparkling. "Jonah, meet Blackie."

Jonah reached out his hand to let the horse snuffle it. "Sorry, man," he said. "I didn't bring any treats. Maybe next time." He scratched along Blackie's neck, and the horse tilted his head to give the man access to his ears.

"You ride?" LeeAnn asked.

"Oh, yeah," Jonah replied. "Some of the places I survey, it's the only way to get back to the areas we need to check out. At least at first, anyway."

When her back stiffened, he cursed himself for speaking without thinking. Of course she wouldn't want to hear how Natural Shale built inroads across the land they drilled.

How to get this conversation back on track?

"How long have you had this guy?" he asked, working to keep his tone light. He knew how to put people at ease. It was part of what made him good at the negotiation parts of his job.

Conversational. That's the ticket.

"Since I was fifteen. He was a rescue. Way too many horses get abandoned in Texas. People think they want a horse when what they really want is a pet. They think it's going to be like a dog—a little food and water, and he's fine. They don't realize the commitment a horse really takes." She paused, glancing at him out of the corner of her eye, as if gauging his reaction to her mini rant. When he kept his gaze level and his expression interested, she continued in a more moderate tone. "Anyway, Gran took in horses all the time, rehabbed them, found good homes for them when she could. But when she brought in this pair of black geldings, my cousin Sami and I wouldn't let her give them away. We named them Shadow and Blackie and spent every spare minute with them. Blackie was mine from the moment I saw him." Her voice softened as she reached up to ruffle his mane. "Or maybe I was his."

"Where's Shadow now?"

"He was quite a bit older than Blackie. He died a few years ago." Though her tone stayed steady, she bit her bottom lip and blinked several times as if to hold back tears.

"So did you keep up your grandmother's horse-rescuing tradition?" Jonah regretted the question immediately when her face fell even further.

"No," she said. "I couldn't afford it. Too many vet fees. Too much work."

"But you miss it," he said, his tone a question, even though he could see the answer in her face.

"Yeah. I miss it." She stared at Blackie for a moment, stroking her hand down his neck, then straightened her shoulders.

"Okay," she said. "Let's get started on this search."

Back to business. Right.

"Sounds good to me," he said.

"You really think you're ready for this?" LeeAnn asked.

Jonah shrugged. "Sure. It can't be that bad. Where should we begin?"

That same impish grin lit up her face again. "I'll let you decide," she said. "Come on. I'll show you what we've got to work with."

Uh-oh. That evil smile does not bode well.

What had he gotten himself into?

Chapter Nine

"You have got to be kidding me." Jonah peered into the dim recesses of the oldest outbuilding on the ranch—a wooden structure that creaked ominously, even in the gentle breeze that fluttered by. Giant cobwebs festooned the corners, and a thick coating of dust lay across the piles of broken chairs, old desks, and rotting trunks. "I'm beginning to think 'hoarder' was an understatement."

Behind him, LeeAnn snickered. She pulled a pair of leather work gloves out of her back pocket. "Now you see why I don't know where the paperwork is," she said.

"How many more of these buildings are there?" Jonah asked. He could see another barn off in the distance, and what looked like some old stables with peeling red paint.

"Of the ones I haven't gone through yet? There are three barns, a stable, two attics, and a storm cellar." Tucking her hair up more firmly under the straw hat she wore, LeeAnn moved past him to step inside. There didn't seem to be any real path, so Jonah followed her as she picked her way past tottering heaps of junk.

"You know," he began conversationally, "I thought I'd seen everything. This isn't the first time I've had to search for paperwork. I've had to sort through old storage units, attics, basements." He paused to watch dust motes dancing in a beam of sunlight falling through a crack in the wall. "But I've never seen anything quite like this."

"Well, at least it will give me a chance to see what's in these buildings," LeeAnn said. "I'd love to find something valuable—go on one of those antique-appraisal shows and discover that some piece of junk is worth a fortune."

"What would you do with it?" He lifted the edge of a square piece of plywood and peered under it.

Her voice floated back to him as she moved behind a stack of mismatched chairs. "Split it with my cousins. Their dad blew all their inheritance in the stock market, then died of a heart attack before he could recoup any of it. I'd love to be able to make sure they got something." When she popped back into sight, she had a smudge of dirt across her nose. "There are several trunks back here—one of them has papers in it, but I can't tell what they are. Want to start here, or do you want to see the other buildings first?"

He thought about it for a second. "Let's take a quick tour so I can get a sense of exactly what we're facing."

If the rest of the buildings were anything like this one, he had his work cut out for him.

By noon, Jonah was convinced that he should have insisted

another landman take this particular job, promotion or no promotion. He was also pretty sure that no one but LeeAnn would have taken a job as his assistant.

And I practically had to blackmail her.

Usually, tracking down mineral rights was a typical research job—he could find the answers he needed in local courthouse records. Occasionally he had to sort through a filing cabinet.

Nothing like this.

LeeAnn had been right. As far as he could tell, each of the outbuildings had been filled up with junk—in no particular order—then locked up and all but abandoned.

His head ached from inhaling dust and mildew for the last few hours.

All they had discovered was that there were probably thousands of pieces of paper in trunks and boxes, any one of which could hold the information they needed. The stables, in particular, seemed to hold an extraordinary number of cardboard boxes labeled simply "records."

"Let me get this straight," LeeAnn said, climbing into his truck for the short drive back up to the main house from the outbuilding at the farthest edge of the ranch. "Any mention of mineral rights being willed to someone could be the basis for a potential legal wrangle? It doesn't have to be filed at the courthouse or anything?" She blew an errant strand of hair out of her eyes, and a puff of dust followed it.

"Right. It's harder to prove and less definitive, but with mineral rights, sometimes that's all it takes for someone else to end up with the legal right to drill."

She shook her head, her lips twisting up. "It's going to take ages to go through everything. You really sure your company's going to think this is the best use of your time?"

He didn't miss the sneer in her voice when she said "your company," but he ignored it. "I'm going to call them. My guess is yes, though—they want to drill here."

Surprisingly enough, Jonah found himself hoping he was right. Although he didn't relish the thought of spending hours digging through the dusty, old outbuildings, the idea of spending more time with LeeAnn was oddly enticing. Even covered in dust, she was absolutely beautiful. In fact, he had spent more time watching her as she bent over to pull out boxes than he cared to admit. He had to keep reminding himself that she saw him as the enemy—and that as lovely as she might be, they were on opposing sides of this issue.

Hippies, man. You don't want any part of that bullshit.

But he couldn't help a covert, admiring glance at the way her breasts pushed forward when she put her hands on her hips and leaned backward, stretching out her back. "Ready for a break?" she asked.

"Sure." He stood up and dusted off his jeans. "I'll call my boss before we do anything else. And then tomorrow—"

"No, tomorrow's Sunday," LeeAnn interrupted, shaking her head. "We can work again on Monday, but I'm not teaching, and I've got things to do around the ranch tomorrow."

"Sounds like a plan," Jonah replied, pulling his cell phone out of his pocket and heading downstairs.

More time with LeeAnn. What could it possibly hurt?

Chapter Ten

Monday morning, Jonah leaned against the door frame, one booted foot crossed over the other. He had expected Lee-Ann's morning class to be finished, but he was suddenly glad it wasn't. She sat at the front of the room, her legs crossed, eyes closed, hands folded in prayer position as she murmured to the class, encouraging them to relax one muscle at a time. The soothing sound of her voice seemed to move right through him, and he felt his shoulders loosen. He could listen to her voice forever.

The thought jerked him straight up, and he muffled a curse as he bumped his elbow against the door frame.

Not forever.

He was here to do a job. That was all.

And once this job was over, he would be gone again.

Fort Worth wasn't home. He had an apartment out in Midland, but he mostly lived in hotel rooms, moving to follow the jobs as they showed up. Of course, the quality of the lodgings had improved dramatically since he had first started his career—careful investment in the gas and oil industry he had learned inside and out meant that he was wealthy enough in his own right, at this point—but none of the places he stayed were home.

And if some tiny part of him regretted that? He didn't have to pay attention to it.

LeeAnn's soft announcement that the students should begin to sit up drew his focus back to her. She glanced up at him through the door, her gaze steady. Then she turned back to the class and bowed over her hands. "Namaste," she said.

She stood up in one fluid motion and waved him into the room. More than one woman paused to stare at him as the students streamed by him on their way out of the room.

"Why are you here?" Her tone was suspicious. "Aren't we supposed to meet at the ranch?"

"I thought maybe we could ride out together. Then you could bring me back when you come in for your evening class."

She bent over to roll up her mat. "I don't want you to feel stranded out there."

The sight of her ass in the air as she gathered up her belongings hit him low in the belly, and he had to clear his voice before he could speak again. What had they been discussing? Oh. Right. "No worries." His voice turned wry as he considered the state of the outbuildings. "I'll have plenty to keep me busy."

With a shrug, she stood up straight. "Okay. Meet me out in the lobby in fifteen minutes. There's chai tea out there if you want some."

Never in his life had he met a woman who could actually

be ready in fifteen minutes. Jonah settled into one of the brown leather chairs grouped around a small coffee table near the entryway and blew the steam across the top of the paper cup he had filled from the dispenser. Really, he preferred coffee, but at least it kept him busy for a moment. Better than reading any of the yoga magazines on the table in front of him.

Though some of those stretches were amazing. He began flipping through the one closest to him, but with every page, he imagined LeeAnn, bent over, stretched out, strong and lithe. It was only a small step from that to thinking of her in those same positions, naked, smiling over her shoulder at him.

Dammit.

He had to get control of himself.

Just a job.

That's all she was.

A bit of a nutjob, at that. Anyone who does yoga whenever she gets anxious has to be a little crazy.

He imagined her bent over, hands on the floor.

He shifted in the seat, uncomfortably aware of the throb of his sudden erection.

So of course that was the moment she walked into the room.

"Ready to go?" she asked brightly. She couldn't have been gone for more than ten minutes. Her hair, still damp from a shower, spilled across her shoulders, and her face had been scrubbed clean.

She was absolutely beautiful.

"Sure," he said, his voice gruff. "Give me a second." He practically dived into the men's locker room, then leaned against the closed door and breathed deeply.

If her mere presence affected him this strongly, how was he going to continue to spend day after day with her? Those buildings were stuffed with decades' worth of papers. Really, he needed a full team to sort through them.

Work. He had to concentrate on work.

He could do this.

After another moment, he blew out a breath and rubbed his hands across his face. Then he pulled open the door and met LeeAnn's puzzled glance with a smile. "Let's go," he said.

. . .

"Where do you want to start today?" LeeAnn asked, glancing at Jonah out of the corner of her eye. He'd grabbed a gym bag out of his truck and locked it up, choosing to ride over in LeeAnn's car. Just as well—her Prius was the better environmental option, anyway. But she had to admit, he looked a little out of place, his broad shoulders eclipsing the small seat and the top of his cowboy hat brushing the ceiling of the interior.

"Do you have any ideas in particular? Places your grandmother might have stored paperwork connected to the land?" His navy blue eyes stared at her steadily.

"Hmm. I have two answers to that. There were a lot of boxes of papers in one of the guest bedrooms. Gran closed the door and put a bookcase in front of it before I was even born, I think—I never remember it being open. Those records are probably go up to the 1980s or '90s? But I have no idea how far back they go—through Gran's lifetime, probably, though I can't be certain. Those are in the attic. The other place I'm certain has papers is the barn—there's a stack of trunks with old records of some sort." She shrugged. "So really, it's up to you."

Pulling open the car door, she stepped out into the spring heat. Jonah followed.

"One more question, then," Jonah said from behind her. "I told you why I hired you. So why are you helping me search? There's no guarantee that we won't find something you don't like. Why let me go through the records at all?"

Why, indeed?

Pausing on the bottom step leading up to the porch, she considered her words carefully, then moved up to sit on the porch swing. Jonah took one of the chairs across from her, leaning over with his elbows on his knees, hands clasped loosely between his legs, eyes intent upon her face.

"Here's the deal. That guy I was trying to avoid in the diner the other day? My ex, like I told you." She paused, half expecting some smart-ass comment, but he didn't interrupt. "When we split up, it was ugly. Really horrible—primarily because he lied to me, had been lying to me for months, maybe even years. By the time he broke up with me, he was already engaged to someone else."

A nod from Jonah encouraged her to continue.

She stared out at the field to the east of the house, covered in newly blooming bluebonnets. "It's not the first time I've been lied to. When I was a child…" She shook her head. "Anyway, suffice to say I'm not a fan of lies. Not even by omission. If I didn't do at least the bare minimum to help you find out who owns that right? It would be a lie. I'm not willing to do that."

Jonah's snort drew her attention back to him. "I think sorting through all the crap your grandmother had in storage counts as more than the bare minimum."

With a laugh, she stood up. "You're probably right. But I can't be the person I want to be if I don't do it."

When he frowned, a crease appeared between his eyebrows, making her want to reach out and smooth it away. "What does that mean?"

She fought down the urge to touch him. "It means that if I don't help you search, I'll forever feel like I'm living a lie."

"Okay, then," he replied. "Let's get started. I think the attic first."

"It's this way." She opened the door, leading him into the cool, shaded interior.

With any luck at all, they would find something that proved she owned the mineral rights.

Then he would go.

Suddenly, she wasn't entirely sure she wanted luck to be on her side.

Not quite yet, anyway.

Chapter Eleven

Three hours later, Jonah stretched, leaning backward until his spine made small popping noises. "Anything?" he asked.

"No." LeeAnn pulled her attention from the cord of muscle along his forearms and waved her hands at the piles of papers surrounding her. "But some of this stuff is amazing. I've got a whole stack of love letters here to Gran from her husband, from before they were married."

"Be sure to skim those," he said. "Even a written comment about intention can make a difference in the strength of your case."

"Or yours." She extended one arm above her head, then the other, shaking out the kinks that had developed after hours of sitting.

"Right." Jonah's reply was distracted as he pulled another box off the top of the stack next to him. A beam of light from the dormer window above highlighted a blue gleam in his hair—one that matched his eyes almost perfectly. The jacket he'd had on that morning lay across another box, the cowboy hat atop it. Dust streaked the gray T-shirt that stretched across his chest. More dirt showed where he had wiped his fingers on his thighs. When he bent over to sift through an open container, an upside-down handprint showed on the back of his jeans.

That perfect backside.

Wow, he looks good in jeans.

The night before, LeeAnn had done her own online searching through records, and after finding a number of entries about his work as a landman, she'd also pulled up a high school yearbook picture of Jonah. For some reason, that had fascinated her.

He had definitely come into his own sometime after graduation. The picture was of a cute kid with the same dark hair and eyes—but without the broad shoulders and defined muscles. And definitely without the smoldering sensuality that simmered under the surface of the man in front of her.

With a start, she realized that she had been staring too long and moved to open another dusty cardboard box.

He was far too distracting for her own good.

• • •

LeeAnn had been watching him for several minutes, and it took everything he had not to move over and sweep her up into his arms right then. But that would be a terrible idea. Unprofessional, at best—and at worst? He paused in his work, considering that. What could be the worst possible outcome? She hadn't said as much, but she was still dealing with the fallout from her broken relationship with that idiot at the diner. What's his name—the man slut. If he tried to seduce her now, he would be the rebound guy. He wasn't interested in something that temporary.

But he could wait. And sticking around to look through her pack rat grandmother's buildings gave him the perfect excuse.

It had taken more than a little persuading to get Nathan to agree to pay him for his time for this. But they both knew this deal could end up being big. Getting it would land Jonah his promotion and give Nathan a boost up into senior management.

It wasn't like his entire career was riding on this one drilling-rights deal—but it wasn't all that far off from it, either.

It also gave him an excellent reason to stick around.

That business about her refusal to lie gave him a twinge, though. Would using this search as a reason to spend time with her set off that lie detector of hers?

It didn't matter. No way in hell was he going to pass up this chance to spend as much time with her as possible.

The thought made him pause. What was he up to, here?

Sure, he wanted to find the drilling rights, and if they belonged to LeeAnn, try to convince her to lease them out to Natural Shale.

And he definitely wanted the promotion.

But he had never gone to these lengths before to try to get access to a property, even back when he was starting out and hungry to make a name in the business.

There was something about LeeAnn that drew him. Some part of him wanted to find an excuse to be here, to allow her to get to know him.

Out of the corner of his eye, he saw LeeAnn shake herself and begin sorting through another box.

With a grin, he began reading a postcard sent to her grandmother in the 1950s.

Fine. He could admit it to himself, even if he never said it aloud to anyone else.

I am in no hurry to finish.

. . .

The only thing that made spending the morning digging through stacks of crap worth the aggravation was watching Jonah come to the realization that there was no organizational method at all. Items had been simply grabbed at random, shoved into a box, and added to the stacks. When an outbuilding was full, Gran had closed it off and padlocked it, and rarely opened it again. No one ever believed LeeAnn when she tried to explain the extent of Gran's hoarding—but she suspected Jonah might have a better understanding of it now.

On the plus side, she had found a couple of small treasures today—a gold-colored brooch covered with tiny seed pearls that Sami would love, and a postcard of the Fort Worth Stockyards from the 1940s that, once framed, would make a great addition to the decor in Cowbelles. She could give it to Kylie for her birthday.

But no sign of anything about mineral rights.

Finding nothing meant that Jonah would be around even longer, and she wasn't sure how she felt about that. His wry commentary as they made their way from one cluttered building to the next had made her laugh out loud in a way that no one had since before she found out about Darrell's secret fiancée.

That was a problem.

She needed to be able to see Jonah as the enemy.

He was there to find a way to drill on her land, with or without her permission.

That land was the last connection she had to her gran, the woman who had been her refuge when her parents died, who had taught her how to ride a horse, to mend a fence, to care for the land she would eventually inherit.

Her gran would not have approved of anyone drilling. She was certain of it.

Even more than that, though, the ranch was LeeAnn's stability, her safety. Even when the rest of her world was falling apart around her, she could pull on her boots, saddle Blackie, and take off across the pasture toward the low, rolling hills, and everything bad dropped away. Keeping the land safe was like keeping her heart safe.

So she would protect it.

Straightening her shoulders, she poured tea over ice and carried the glasses out to the living room, where Jonah stood examining the family photos she had framed on the wall.

"I didn't want to get the furniture dirty," he said, waving his hand over his dust-covered jeans.

"Let's go on the porch, then." She led the way, choosing the cushioned wicker porch swing. Jonah lowered himself onto the seat next to her, pushing against the porch with the heel of his boot enough to set the swing into motion.

"There's one thing I don't understand," he said, leaning back onto the cushioned seat.

"Mmm?" She sipped her drink, the cold tea washing away the dust that had gathered in her throat while they worked.

"If you're so opposed to lying that you're willing to risk learning that you don't actually own the mineral rights—to risk having someone come in and drill on your property, in order to avoid telling a lie?" He paused.

"Yes?"

"Then what was that kiss in the Wagon Wheel?" His Clark Kent dimples flashed as he grinned at her, waiting expectantly.

With her surprised laugh, she inhaled a mouthful of tea, choking on it for a brief moment as she flailed for an answer.

"That *was* a lie, right?" he asked.

Was it? Her response had certainly been real enough. But he was right—she had kissed him to send a message to Darrell. And that message was a lie.

It didn't have to be.

"Yeah. I guess it was a lie," she said.

"So why is that different from searching for mineral rights records?" Stretching one arm along the back of the swing behind her, he tilted his head. His navy blue eyes regarded her intently. From anyone else, that kind of scrutiny would have made her nervous.

But she found that for the first time ever, she wanted to tell someone about the reason for her aversion to lies.

Even if I've known him for only a few days.

The thought startled her. Somehow, it already seemed longer.

But maybe if he knew what drove her, he would...what? Decide her feelings were more important than doing his job?

Unlikely.

Still, she found herself wanting to make him really

understand.

Even if he's the enemy.

Maybe because he was the enemy.

Her response came slowly, long pauses punctuating her words. "I lived with my gran when I was a teenager, after my parents died."

He nodded. "I read about the accident. Their car was hit by a train, right?"

"Yeah. Stalled out on the tracks—the conductor wasn't able to stop in time. No way it could have been avoided." She stared down the driveway, noting the yellow and white wildflowers blooming alongside the caliche road. "That's what they told me at the time, anyway."

"But that wasn't the truth?" His voice was gentle.

"No." She shook her head. "I didn't know for years, but apparently my uncle George found a letter—a suicide note." A harsh laugh escaped her. "I guess you'd call it a suicide-murder note? Anyway. It wasn't an accident. Dad planned it."

"Oh, LeeAnn. I am so sorry." His arm descended around her shoulders, drawing her close. She leaned into him.

"It's okay—as okay as it can ever be, anyway. Gran was devastated, too, of course. But I never really forgave Uncle George for not telling us sooner." The warmth of his hand seeped through the sleeve of her T-shirt and into her upper arm.

He made a low noise—of encouragement or understanding, or maybe both.

"I discovered yoga not long after I learned the truth. It was good for me, gave me an outlet for the anger and pain I was feeling, a way to process all those negative emotions.

Between that and helping Gran on the ranch, I finally...I guess I found peace again."

"Understandable."

"That's also when I realized that the principles of yoga could help me figure out my own values—and that they were remarkably similar to the things Gran taught me on the ranch. Respect the earth, don't cause harm when I can avoid it—"

He tilted his head to glance down at her. "Don't lie?"

"Yes, though that comes in under not causing harm."

"Hmm." He paused, almost as if he wasn't going to speak at all, then continued anyway. "So that's when you started doing yoga anytime you're nervous or upset?"

She felt her face flame. "I didn't realize it was that obvious."

"I don't know how you could think anyone might miss it." The smile in his voice took some of the sting out of his words.

Not that it matters what he thinks.

She shook her head to try to dismiss the thought and tried to make her tone light. "Anyway. That's why I don't lie."

Usually.

"And the kiss doesn't count?" His breath ruffled her hair and she could hear the smile in his voice.

"It probably should. But I wasn't thinking of it that way." She spoke quietly.

"How were you thinking of it?" he asked, his tone matching hers.

"I wasn't really thinking at all. I was enjoying it." She held her breath, waiting for his response.

Instead of speaking, he turned to face her in the seat, staring into her eyes. Gently, he reached out and brushed his knuckle down her cheek. "Me, too," he whispered. "Me, too."

Chapter Twelve

Back in the attic, LeeAnn tried to concentrate on the box of papers in front of her. She held a wad of papers in her hand, her head bent down over them, but she wasn't really seeing them at all.

What had that been on the porch? A caress? A simple acknowledgment?

The buzz of her phone interrupted LeeAnn's circling thoughts, and she picked it up perhaps more thankfully than she might have at another time, checking the caller's ID before she clicked over to talk.

"Hey, Sami," she said. "What's up?"

The staticky, garbled reply made her stand up. "I'm in the attic—reception here is terrible. Hang on a sec, okay?" Jonah nodded when she tilted her head to let him know she was headed downstairs, and it wasn't until she was on the second-floor landing that she realized she still had that stack of papers in her hand. Moving into her bedroom, she set them down on the antique oak bedside table.

"You still there?" she asked, eyeing the quilt that covered her four-poster bed. Better not sit there—she'd be sure to leave it covered in dust.

"Yeah. I wanted to know if I could have a get-together at your house tonight." Sami's voice was half eager, half anxious.

"Tonight? A little short notice."

"I know, I know. But it's for a good cause—I promise." Sami's voice turned wheedling.

I know that tone.

"What have you done this time, Sami?" she asked.

Her cousin's sigh sounded almost defeated—unusual for Sami. "I'll tell you all about it at the party. After your yoga class, maybe? We could use the fire pit in the backyard, maybe do some grilling."

LeeAnn's mouth twisted. "Grilling meat?"

"We'll bring our own wire rack. I swear, it won't touch any of your vegetables."

She snorted. "Okay, fine. But only if you promise to call Kylie, too. She and Cole just got home."

Sami's squeal made her pull the phone from her ear. "I love Cole," her cousin said gleefully.

"Yeah, yeah. Make sure your friends know that he's off duty. No fangirling."

"Got it. Okay. No problem. I'll be there at five to set up. Ciao." Sami clicked off.

LeeAnn shook her head and glanced around her room. At least she wouldn't have to clean house before her unexpected guests showed up. She had scrubbed practically every inch of the old farmhouse before Jonah arrived on the first day they'd spent searching through Gran's things.

Anyway, she didn't expect any of them to venture farther indoors than the half bath off the living room.

But she would have to clean herself up, covered as she was in dust and cobwebs.

Resisting the urge to run her fingers through her ponytail, she headed back upstairs to invite Jonah to join Sami's mostly impromptu party.

After all, it was the polite thing to do. It's what Gran would have done.

It would also let her keep an eye on the enemy.

That's what she told herself, anyway—even if deep down, she knew that really, she wanted him to stick around a little longer.

• • •

When LeeAnn told him she needed to gather wood for the party and he offered to help, Jonah had envisioned traipsing out to a woodpile, maybe beside the barn, and gathering up armloads of logs to take to the backyard. "Bring your gloves," she had said.

He hadn't anticipated walking right past that building, stopping only long enough for LeeAnn to grab an ax hanging up on the wall right inside the barn door. "You carry that," she said, pointing at a large gray plastic trash can. When he glanced inside, it was empty, so with a shrug, he hooked it with one hand and carried it behind him, over one shoulder. They continued down to a small copse of gnarled mesquite trees at the back of the old pasture that took up the southwestern corner of the ranch.

The scrubby trees had grown up and around the fencing that separated the pasture from the rest of the land, thorny branches pushing at the wire until they pulled the fence posts over at an angle.

As he watched, LeeAnn lifted the ax, ready to take a swing at one of the smaller trees. "You want me to do that?" he asked.

"Nope," she said. "I want you to see if you can break off some of the smaller branches closer to the fence—that part actually takes more upper-body strength." She followed through with her swing, her ponytail flipping back and forth with the motion.

Surprised by how much he enjoyed watching her—the combined athleticism, grace, and economy of her movements tugging again at a place that seemed to draw on both his chest and his stomach—Jonah moved to follow her directions, carefully disentangling the branches from the fence before twisting and breaking them off.

Sometimes he called her over to use the hand ax on some of the larger branches, but for the most part, they worked in companionable silence.

Finally, though, he asked, "Do we need to pick up some kindling, too?"

"It wouldn't hurt." Toeing the dried, fallen branches with her boot, she said, "The green's better for smoking and adding flavor, of course, but we'll need some that will burn a little quicker." She swung at a half-felled tree, bracing her boot against the trunk to pull out the ax. A loud *pop* as she kicked at it again announced the final crack of the small tree trunk. As the tree fell over, the branch he had grabbed to twist off ripped out of his hands, the sharp thorns slicing at his wrists before he could jerk away, biting deeply into the right one and ripping the skin.

"Oh, no." LeeAnn dropped the ax to the ground and reached out to grab his injured arm.

"It's okay," he said, but one sight of the blood welling up along the deep scratch that snaked up from the top of his glove to the bottom of his rolled-up shirt sleeve had LeeAnn pulling off the bandanna she kept tied around her hat.

Her touch was light, but she tied the pink cloth tightly around the wound as she said, "We at least need to clean it." She glanced around the ground at the tree they had felled. "Let's take what we can and head back to the house. Sami can get the rest if she wants it."

Less than ten minutes of loading branches and twigs into the trash can, and it was full. Their load included much of the main trunk of the short tree, even—once it was down, LeeAnn had managed to chop off most of the remaining branches fairly quickly.

His offer to help chop had again been declined—this time due to his injury. "But if you promise to use only your left hand, you can pull the can home," LeeAnn said, nodding toward the now-unwieldy gray container, full of twisted branches sticking up into the air. "It's got wheels, but they're not always that great over this terrain." She grinned and stepped out to lead the way.

Jonah was happy to follow behind her. Even the pain in his arm, now faded from a sharp slice to a relatively dull ache, couldn't distract him from the way her hips moved as she walked in front of him.

Being outside, working on her ranch, suited her. Even her walk seemed happy.

An echoing joy swirled inside him.

How could he possibly take that away from her?

I'm not. I'm helping her find a way to keep her land.

He glanced back at the small stand of mesquite.

Right in the middle of the plat that Natural Shale had pegged to drill.

If they found the evidence he hoped for, she wouldn't keep those trees. Even if she kept the land.

There are other stands of mesquite.

He was almost sure he'd seen some in the northeast corner of the ranch, out by the horse's pasture. It's not like they were an endangered species. The damn trees were ubiquitous in Texas.

They're practically an invasive *species.*

But no matter how he twisted it around in his mind, he couldn't dissolve the lump that had formed in the pit of his stomach.

He couldn't help but notice that since they'd started working together on the ranch, she hadn't once fallen into doing yoga—not even when they were combing through her grandmother's stored belongings.

This is where she's comfortable.

Where she can be herself.

With his uninjured arm, he pulled the wheeled garbage can full of mesquite across the slightly rocky land toward the house. Turning backward to guide it more precisely through a particularly rough section, he found himself working to move the wheels around a patch of wildflowers, rather than allowing the delicate blue and white petals to be crushed.

Oh, yeah. I'm definitely in trouble.

Chapter Thirteen

Settling back into the white plastic lawn chair LeeAnn had pulled out from a small shed right behind the house, Jonah took a long pull on the Shiner beer her cousin Sami had handed him and let his gaze drift across the backyard.

But not to LeeAnn.

Not immediately, anyway.

Instead, he watched as people came around from where they parked their cars, clearly comfortable making their way to the backyard without anyone to guide them. Obviously, this kind of get-together was fairly common among her friends.

He'd helped Sami drag a Styrofoam ice chest over to the enormous black grill and pull out various packages wrapped in butcher paper. Then another woman brought around some sort of wire mesh that stretched across half of the bottom shelf of the grill. She and Sami carefully unwrapped the meat and set it out to cook on the lowest shelf, while a third friend took care of brushing it with some sort of spice-and-oil mix.

From the conversation he overheard as he helped monitor the mesquite wood he added to the grill, he ascertained that LeeAnn wanted the meat and the vegetables cooked separately.

She's a vegetarian? Figures.

Still, she wasn't complaining about the other people at the party having steak. Even now, the beautiful yoga instructor was nodding at something Sami said, and taking over for the woman brushing barbecue sauce over the meat.

Willing to prepare food she refused to eat, only to please her guests?

What does that say about what truly matters to her?

Jonah finished off the Shiner and switched the empty bottle to his injured hand so he could leverage himself out of the chair. He moved toward the recycling bin LeeAnn had set out around the side of the house nearest the grill two hours earlier, right after she finished cleaning and bandaging his wound.

She had insisted on taking care of him herself, her fingers gently probing the deep scratch as she ran it under warm water in the kitchen.

Part of him had wanted to insist that the cut wasn't that bad—but the part that was enjoying the attention won out as he watched the way she tilted her head and peered at his wrist.

The touch of her hands on his skin had sent a frisson of electricity up his arm, even as the soap and water burned against the gash in his skin.

As he bent over to set the bottle in the green bin,

LeeAnn's voice floated over him as she quizzed Sami in near whispers. "Wait. Your boss is your boyfriend?"

"He was." Sami's tone was more than a little defensive.

"Your boyfriend is *married*?" The whisper turned to a hiss as LeeAnn injected the last word with a cross of horror and disgust.

"I didn't know." Sami sounded close to tears.

I don't want to hear this.

But he couldn't bring himself to stop listening.

"Oh, sweetie." LeeAnn's voice turned gentle. "You've got to stop falling for your bosses. This is what? Number three? It never turns out well. You trust too easily."

"I can't be like you, never trusting anyone at all."

"That's not true." LeeAnn sounded more shocked than upset by the claim. "I trust people all the time. I trust *you* completely." A slight pause made the next comment less believable than it might have been otherwise. "I trusted Darrell."

Sami snorted. "No, you didn't. You chose him because he was so clearly *un*trustworthy, he was bound to prove you right. You think you can't trust anyone but yourself."

Jonah rocked back on his heels, so absorbed in hearing what LeeAnn said next that he almost forgot he was eavesdropping.

He wished he could see LeeAnn's face. What was her reaction to her cousin's claims?

But she didn't reply.

"I'm sorry," Sami said. "You don't need this, me psychoanalyzing you when you're dealing with a breakup."

LeeAnn's strained shrug came through her voice. "What I don't need is Darrell—he's a jackass. So is your boss."

"I wouldn't need anyone, either, if I had that new guy on the string. He is *hot*." Sami ended her pronouncement with a hissing, sizzling noise, following LeeAnn's lead back to lighter conversation.

"I don't have anyone on a string," LeeAnn said. "Jonah Hamilton is out to make money by destroying the ranchland—nothing else. I wouldn't have invited him tonight if he hadn't been here when you called."

Even though he already knew what she thought of him, for some reason, her stark evaluation of his motives sent a spike of pain through him.

That's what I get for eavesdropping.

Jonah rattled the bottles in the bin against one another until they clinked loudly enough to announce his presence, then stood up straight and moved around the corner of the house into the backyard. Peering over the top of the grill, he took a deep, appreciative breath of the fragrant mesquite smoke—mostly in order to give the two women time to gather their composure. "So," he said, casually, "what do you suggest?"

Only when LeeAnn answered did he look up at them. "The grilled zucchini," she said. "I'll be putting it out to cook in about five more minutes."

"No way," Sami said, bumping her cousin with her hip. "I think the pork loin is best." Her smile was strained as she aimed for a light tone. "But don't tell anyone, okay? Good Texas girls are supposed to prefer steak."

"Not that you're a good Texas girl," LeeAnn said, raising one eyebrow. Sami gasped, then, catching the upward quirk of the yoga instructor's lip, huffed out a laugh and shook her head.

As he turned to leave, Jonah saw LeeAnn reach down to squeeze her cousin's hand in a gesture of support.

Good. Family matters. Especially when they need you.

Not that LeeAnn's values were important to him.

He was here to do a job, get his promotion, and move on. It was fine to be needed by family, but he didn't need anyone. He sure didn't need a neo-hippie-chick vegetarian. Even if she was beautiful and kind.

I am in no way invested in LeeAnn Walker.

And he could keep telling himself that.

Right up to the point that he arranged for Natural Shale to come drill on her land. That, he feared, would break her heart.

So what are my values?

He shook his head to dislodge the question and moved toward a small group of people LeeAnn had introduced him to when they first arrived.

Before this job, he had been fine. He had known what was important to him—doing the job he was hired to do, moving forward in his career.

Had that changed since he had hired LeeAnn to work with him?

What really matters to me?

And why am I just now asking that question?

• • •

LeeAnn circulated through the party, speaking to her guests, refilling drinks, offering to take empty plates and cups. But by the time it was completely dark, she had pulled up a chair next to Sami at the fire pit, planning to take a few moments to relax.

She really wanted to quiz Sami more about the situation with her boss, but the close call with Jonah earlier had convinced her it was a bad idea—she knew her cousin wouldn't want anyone to know that she had been tricked into having an illicit affair.

So instead, she stared contemplatively into the fire dancing in front of her until the sweep of headlights turning into her driveway snagged her attention. "Think that's Kylie and Cole?" she asked Sami.

"No. Kylie said she didn't think they'd make it. Sounded like they had other plans." Sami smirked as she downed the last of one of the tiny bottles of moscato wine she had brought. The firelight glinted off the several necklaces she wore layered over a purple sixties-style mod dress and black leggings.

Setting her own beer down on the grass beside her chair, LeeAnn stood. "I'll see who it is—be back in a minute." Sami waved an acknowledgment and pulled her knees up to her chest, wrapping her arms around her knees.

I can't believe Sami's jerk of a boss is married.

Or that my boyfriend was engaged to someone else.

Had Jonah really overheard their conversation at the grill, or was she worrying about nothing?

Why would it matter if he did hear me talking about him? It's not like he doesn't know what I think of him.

But as she rounded the corner of the house toward the front drive, she found herself considering the possibility that her opinion of Jonah Hamilton might have begun to change.

So what do I really think of him?

Any possible answer to that question was wiped out of

her mind when she saw who was climbing out of the silver
SUV at the back of the informally parked cars scattered
across the yard.

Darrell Vincent.

What is that lying, cheating jerk doing here?

· · ·

Jonah only half listened to the tall redhead talking to him
about the value of proper breathing—a friend of LeeAnn's
from the yoga studio, he assumed. She was nice enough, and
any other time he would probably be flirting. But somewhat
to his surprise, he wasn't interested in anything she had to
offer.

*So would I be willing to pay attention to LeeAnn talking
about breathing techniques? Yes. Absolutely.*

His answer surprised him in its vehemence. He had to
fight the urge to shake his head in dismay—it wouldn't be
polite to the woman in front of him.

*Ah, Hamilton. You dumbass. You heard LeeAnn—she
thinks you're only out for cash.*

Where was she, anyway? Several moments before, he
had seen her stand up and head toward the front of the
house. But she hadn't returned.

He smiled politely at the redhead, waiting for a break in
the conversation. "Excuse me," he said, touching her fore-
arm to soften any possible offense. "I need to go check on
our hostess."

The woman—*Hannah? Anna? Something like that*—
smiled thinly but nodded. "Of course."

He heard LeeAnn's voice as he rounded the corner.

"You're not invited," she was saying. "Get back in your car and go away."

From behind, LeeAnn's entire body radiated tension, her muscles bunched as if preparing for flight. A man stood close to her, his sandy brown hair flopped forward to obscure his face as he spoke in a low rumble. Jonah couldn't make out the words, but he recognized the tone—wheedling.

"Everything okay here?" Jonah asked, stepping forward and tilting his hat back a little.

When the man glanced up, Jonah recognized him from the newspaper.

Darrell Vincent. The dumbass who dumped her.

LeeAnn turned around, and Vincent took the opportunity to slip his arm around her waist and pull her in close to him. She flinched away but didn't pull herself entirely out of his grip.

"Everything's fine," Vincent said.

Jonah shook his head. "Don't think so, man. I heard the lady say you weren't invited."

"This has nothing to do with you," Vincent said. "It's between me and *the lady*. Go on back to the party. Get lost."

At the ugly emphasis in Vincent's tone, LeeAnn stepped away from him at last. Jonah didn't take his gaze off his opponent, but out of the corner of his eye, he saw her lift up one leg and wrap it around behind the other, then thread her arms around one another and clasp her hands together under her chin. Balancing on one foot, she stared at them with wide eyes.

This creep has her literally twisted up over him.

A cold rage filled Jonah at the thought, wiping out all other considerations. His hands balled into fists, and the rest of the world dropped away as he took a steady, threatening step toward the idiot who had hurt LeeAnn.

· · ·

As Jonah paced steadily forward to loom over Darrell, LeeAnn dropped her foot to the ground and stood planted, as if she were one of the pecan trees in the old grove out in the eastern pasture.

I am absolutely opposed to violence.

So what if a thrill ran through a tiny piece of her heart at the idea of Jonah stepping in to protect her from Darrell?

It doesn't matter.

I have to stop them.

The expression on Jonah's face almost kept her from intervening. It was like nothing she'd seen from him before—dark, forbidding, violent.

He continued to move forward as Darrell scrambled back, the smaller man not quite willing to take his eyes off the menace striding toward him.

Jonah moves like a predator.

In all their interactions, his movements had been controlled and deliberate—designed, she now suspected, to put her at ease.

Is this what he's like underneath the dimples and charm?

His gaze on Darrell remained fierce and intense.

Dangerous.

At the thought, a shiver ran down her spine, even as she hurried to step between them, turning her back to Darrell and placing a palm lightly on Jonah's chest.

"Please don't." Her voice came out steady and strong,

though quiet.

At least I don't sound as shaky as I feel.

Jonah paused, but he didn't take his gaze off his quarry. "He needs to leave."

"I agree." With her other hand, she risked reaching down and grasping one of his bunched fists, even as she realized that he could crush her in an instant.

He would never hurt me.

The thought came unbidden, but strong and certain. Releasing his fist, she skimmed her hand up his arm and placed her fingers against one cheek until he glanced down at her. His navy blue eyes churned with anger.

"He's going." Holding Jonah's gaze with her own, she said more loudly, "You're leaving, Darrell."

The only answer was the slam of the SUV's door. At the sound of the engine starting, LeeAnn risked turning around to watch Darrell drive away. Heat rolled off Jonah, swirling around and up her back.

Part of her wanted to lean into that heat, certain that Jonah would wrap his arms around her.

Protect me.

She shivered.

No violence, she reminded herself. It had no place in her life.

Neither does Jonah Hamilton.

As she moved away from the beckoning warmth of his body to head back to the party, she realized both that she was shaking and that the short altercation had drawn an audience from the partygoers.

"Sami," she said, her voice thin and strained, "make sure the fire is out before everyone leaves?"

Her cousin's brows drew down as her gaze flicked from LeeAnn to Jonah and back. "Of course. You need anything from me?"

"Just make sure everything's put away when the party breaks up." She drew in a deep breath and straightened her shoulders.

"Sure," Sami said as LeeAnn headed inside the house, suddenly too exhausted to try to be a good hostess. It was Sami's party anyway.

And LeeAnn had a lot to consider.

He's not really Superman in a cowboy hat.

He's the enemy, not my protector.

But her hand trembled as she gripped the doorknob, and she could feel Jonah's troubled gaze on her through the closed door behind her.

She stayed awake long after the glow from the fire had been extinguished and the last guest car had pulled away, the headlights sweeping across her bedroom wall. She couldn't be falling for the man who had come to destroy everything she loved.

Could I?

Chapter Fourteen

Swiping her bangs off her forehead, LeeAnn sighed, then bent back over the box she had opened. From across the attic at the top of the farmhouse, Jonah watched her for a minute. "Anything interesting?" he asked.

"No." She sounded discouraged. "Another bunch of old magazines. Day three of searching, and not a single thing about mineral rights or drilling."

When he had arrived at the ranch that morning, LeeAnn made no mention of the party the night before, so he had followed her lead—despite an almost overwhelming urge to explain his actions.

But what could he say? *Sorry, but I needed to murder your ex with my bare hands*? No. That would never do. He couldn't explain it to her.

I can't even explain it to myself.

He'd spent most of the silent ride back to town in Sami's old Audi trying to figure out what had come over him, and he still didn't know why—he only knew that when he saw that jackass Darrell, the urge to protect LeeAnn swelled up in a primal rush of feeling, overwhelming every rational thought.

It was the kind of emotional response that couldn't be expressed in words.

So that leaves work as usual.

Fine. I can do that.

"How old?" He made his way toward her through the narrow path they had created amid the boxes.

"The magazines? Thirties and forties, mostly." She pulled out a stack and thumped them to the floor, then flipped through the covers. "Yeah. A few from the fifties." Another sigh sent up a small flurry of dust, and she sneezed. "As long as we're up here, we might as well start hauling some of this junk out." A quick survey of the attic left her shaking her head. "Or maybe hire a bulldozer."

As Jonah leaned over her shoulder to check out the pile of magazines, she reached up to straighten her pony-tail, leaving streaks of dust in her hair and wafting the smell of her apple-scented shampoo toward him. He closed his eyes momentarily, trying to think of anything other than her body pressed up against him. Or that kiss in the diner. It didn't work, of course, but he pushed the thought aside.

"Were you serious when you talked about finding something in all this stuff to sell for your cousins?" he asked.

"Why? Did you find something?" The graceful curve of her neck as she turned her head to look up at him threatened to distract him again.

LeeAnn wiped her forehead with the back of her wrist, brushing several stray blond hairs out of her eyes, but leaving a streak of dust smudged in their place.

It took all of Jonah's self-control not to gently wipe it away.

What had he been saying?

Oh. Stuff to sell. Right.

"No. Not really," he said, then moved back over to stare down at the magazine he had been searching through. He flipped through the pages, finding nothing, and tossed it into the cardboard box he had designated for completed searches.

There were hundreds of these old magazines. They reminded him of Jenny, a librarian out in West Texas who often helped him track down difficult-to-find information. She was fascinated by print collectibles. She even belonged to some online group—they all helped each other track down stuff like this. The more obscure, the better.

In fact...

He fanned out the stack and stared at it. How obscure were these? He didn't recognize all of the titles, but that really didn't mean anything. With a shrug, he pulled out his phone and snapped a picture. Then he pulled up Jenny's number in his texts, attached the photo, typed, "You interested in anything here?" and hit send.

Couldn't hurt, anyway. Maybe someone would get something out of this wild goose chase.

Since we haven't found anything about mineral rights, and I scared her off by threatening her ex last night.

Blowing out a sigh, he picked up the top magazine from the stack in front of him and riffled through the pages, hoping to find some long-forgotten letter. Preferably one that said something like, *"I hereby bequeath the mineral rights to... to..."*

To whom?

Not LeeAnn. She would never allow Natural Shale to drill on her land.

Who, then?

Some distant cousin? Maybe someone far away. Maine, maybe. Or Idaho. Someone who didn't care about the land. Didn't care if Natural Shale brought in trucks to create makeshift roads crisscrossing LeeAnn's ranch.

Someone who didn't care about the look of misery on her face at the thought of oil riggers crawling all over the land she and Blackie rode every day.

Oh, dammit all to hell, Hamilton.

You stupid son of a bitch. You realize there's no good way for this to end, right?

He glanced up at her, watching the way the rays of sunlight streaked across her face.

Because LeeAnn wasn't the type of woman he could sleep with and then walk away from. Not his usual type at all. He'd known her for only a week, and he already knew that.

You are in some deep shit.

"You okay?" LeeAnn asked, and Jonah realized that his hands had stilled—he was no longer flipping through the magazines and dumping them into the box in the same regular rhythm he had maintained for most of the last hour.

"Fine," he muttered, picking up another magazine, holding it upside down, and shaking it.

Good enough, anyway.

If only he could figure out what to do next.

"You know," she said, "these magazines are in really good shape. I wonder if there's anyone who would be interested in them."

He smiled at the similar tack their minds had taken. "Sure," he said. "There are people out there who would pay good money for some of these old magazines—maybe a lot of money, depending on how rare they are."

She cast a slightly dubious look at the dusty pile in front of her. "Like on eBay?"

He shrugged. "Maybe. You know, a lot of what I do is research, tracking down records in county offices and such. But sometimes I have to go back far enough that I end up in libraries. I have a friend who's a research librarian. If she doesn't know offhand if they're worth anything, she could track it down. If you want her to, that is."

As if he hadn't done the same thing.

"Sure," she said. "Can't hurt, right?"

He pulled his phone out of his pocket and bent over her to fan out this stack of magazines, too. As he did, her shoulder brushed against his side. The contact sent an electric shock through him, and he shivered involuntarily.

He was going to have to get better control of himself— this was supposed to be a job, dammit. No matter how amazing that kiss in the Wagon Wheel had been, she hadn't really meant it. She hadn't been kissing him, not really—she had been showing off for that sleazy ex of hers.

As he snapped a picture of the magazines and tapped out a second quick message to Jenny, he indulged in a brief fantasy of what he'd like to say to the idiot who dumped LeeAnn. But that quickly devolved to a fantasy of what he'd like to *do* to LeeAnn, so he tamped down his imagination again—and the raging erection that threatened to spring up from it.

"There," he said, sending the message and photo out. "I'll let you know what she says."

"Thanks," she said. "You know, if we're really going to be methodical about it, we probably should go ahead and dump the stuff that we know for sure is trash—or at least put labels on the boxes."

"And some of this probably could go out on an auction site, too. People will buy the most amazing junk."

He only barely let himself consider that sorting through the various outbuildings carefully, searching not only for paperwork proving who owned the mineral rights, but for anything at all salable would take more time—time that he could spend getting to know LeeAnn for real.

• • •

That kiss in the diner had been pretty much the most amazing kiss of her life. But LeeAnn was beginning to think that Jonah was regretting it. When he had leaned over her to take the photo, he had accidentally brushed against her shoulder—and had jerked away like she had burned him. Apparently he didn't want to touch her at all, not even accidentally.

She shouldn't feel disappointed at that, but she did.

And that caress of her cheek in the kitchen?

It probably didn't mean anything. He was only saying that he liked kissing.

So he enjoyed the kiss. So what?

"I'll get a marker," she said, standing up and heading toward the narrow staircase leading down into the rest of the house. "We can go through and label all the boxes we've already checked."

"Better yet, let's take a break. I could use a cup of coffee, if you have any." He wiped his hands down the front of his jeans.

Wrinkling her nose and shaking her head, she said, "Sorry. I have some great teas, though. I could brew a pot."

He shrugged. "As long as it's got caffeine, I guess."

"Green tea does. I'll make that." She stood up, then moved through a quick series of stretches, swan diving her torso down so that her nose touched her knees, then up and into a back bend halfway to the floor. When she straightened, she found him watching her intently. Suddenly she felt self-conscious. "Yoga," she said shortly, by way of explanation.

"I guessed." No one ought to be able to put that much amusement into two words.

"I could teach you some moves," she offered.

"Oh, I bet you could." His eyes crinkled at the corners.

Was he teasing? Or ridiculing her?

Dammit. She hadn't felt so awkward in years. Not since she'd been a gawky adolescent, ridiculous and silly. Come to think of it, that might be how he saw her: ridiculous—the type of woman who grabbed a beautiful stranger in public and laid one on him.

Stop thinking, LeeAnn.

She led the way down the stairs, aware of his gaze on her from behind, trying to draw in the kind of deep, calming pranayama yoga breaths she practiced every day. For once, though, focusing on breathing didn't help.

The familiar ritual of brewing tea helped calm her rattled nerves—filling the kettle, rinsing the teapot, spooning tea leaves into the basket, pouring the boiling water into the pot. By the time Jonah joined her in the kitchen, she felt more like herself, serene and in control. The face she turned to him was smooth and pleasant, the one she had practiced showing the rest of the world since Darrell had left. The face that hid any inner turmoil. If she practiced it long enough, she reasoned, perhaps it would eventually become reality.

"Here you go," she said, handing a cup of tea to Jonah. His enormous hand almost entirely engulfed the delicate, rose-patterned china. Turning to the table, she pulled out two chairs and sat down in one of them.

"Let me take you to dinner," Jonah said abruptly.

LeeAnn laughed. "Now?"

"After your class tonight." He took a tentative sip of the tea, then a longer drink—apparently he liked it.

In that moment, she couldn't think of a reason not to go—not unless she wanted to lie. And he was staring at her, waiting for an answer. "Okay," she blurted.

She could have sworn the look on his face was satisfied as he swallowed the rest of the tea in one long drink and stood up.

Wait. I meant no.

Is this a date? What are you up to?

"Good," he said decisively. "Let's get back to work, then."

She gulped down the last of her tea and followed him back upstairs to the attic, scolding herself all the way for not thinking faster.

If it is a date, it's a date with the enemy.

That had to be a bad idea.

Chapter Fifteen

LeeAnn waved at the young woman working the front desk and pushed her way out the door. Her evening class hadn't gone as well as she had hoped it would—she kept finding herself drifting off into thoughts of Jonah, then realizing that she'd left her students in their poses longer than she intended. With any luck, no one had noticed her fractured attention.

But it beat obsessing over Jonah and the not-a-date dinner they were about to have together. Or about Darrell Stupid Loser Vincent and the scene at the ranch the night before.

Why had he been there, anyway?

As she rounded the corner toward the Wagon Wheel, she caught sight of Jonah. He was leaning against the red brick of the building, one boot kicked over the other, staring down at his phone. She paused to watch him in this unguarded moment.

Superman in jeans and a cowboy hat.

A shiver ran through her.

He really is stunning.

Giving herself a mental shake, she picked up her pace again. "Ready?" she asked as she came alongside him.

Those dimples flashed, and her knees quivered.

"Sure." He pulled the door open for her. "I've got some good news, too."

A waitress gathered menus and gestured for them to follow her.

"Good news? About the mineral rights?" Her stomach sank—good news for him meant bad news for her, right?

"No." He waved his phone. "It looks like my friend—the librarian—might know of a buyer for some of those old magazines of your gran's. In fact, she wants us to send her pictures of anything like that that we find."

"Seriously? Someone wants that old junk?" Someone other than Gran, anyway.

"Looks like." Jonah flipped through the pages of the menu, stopping to read descriptions. "You're vegetarian, right? Is it going to bother you if I eat meat?"

"Would it stop you if it did?" She opened her own menu.

"Yes." The surprise in his voice caused her to look up at him. "It's only polite," he said. "But from the look on your face, I'm guessing that hasn't been your experience."

"Not even remotely." Shaking her head, she closed the menu again. "But to answer your question, no, it won't bother me. Vegetarianism is my choice, but I wouldn't force it on anyone else."

"Chicken-fried steak is fine with you?"

"As long as I don't have to eat it." She shrugged. "When

I was little, Gran's land was still a working ranch, cattle and all. I spent time with the cows that ended up on our table."

The waitress came over to take their order, and when she left, Jonah picked up the conversation. "Did hanging out with your dinner when it was still on the hoof influence your decision to become a vegetarian?"

She shook her head. "I didn't think too much about it when I was a kid, but Gran worked with a local slaughterhouse that used more humane methods than some of the big ones." The waitress returned with their iced tea, and LeeAnn picked up the lemon to squeeze it into the glass.

"When did it quit being a working ranch?" Jonah asked.

"Not long after my grandfather died. Gran couldn't run it on her own anymore." She could tell he was about to ask another question, but suddenly she was distracted as the diner door swung open and Darrell pushed in, talking over his shoulder to someone behind him.

"Oh, no," LeeAnn said, interrupting anything Jonah might have been about to say.

Following her gaze to the door, he grimaced. "Checking out the man slut at the door?"

"The very one. And he's here with his fiancée. I cannot get away from him." She closed her eyes and shook her head. "Don't say anything to him." She stared earnestly into Jonah's eyes and reached out to grab one of his hands resting on the table. "I mean it. Not a word."

One corner of Jonah's mouth quirked up. "Okay," he said, drawing the word out. He dropped his other hand on top of hers. "Easy enough."

Cold air rushed over her as Jonah pulled his hand away and stood up.

"What are you doing?" Her voice came out in a hiss.

The slow wink Jonah gave her wasn't reassuring. But he simply moved around and slipped into the booth next to her. The old padding of the seat dipped a little, and Jonah took advantage of her slight lean toward him by dropping an arm around her shoulders and snugging her in tight against him. A zap of electrical heat distracted her for a moment, but didn't keep her from uttering an incoherent sound of surprise.

"I need you to do something for me." He leaned down close enough to her that his breath brushed her cheek when he spoke. "Pretend we're here on a date, okay?"

"A date?" His nearness made her almost dizzy.

"It might convince him to keep his distance." He paused for a second before continuing, his voice turning dangerous, "That would best for everyone concerned."

"Okay." This time she squeaked. Clearing her throat, she tried again. "Yes. Thank you." That warm, spicy scent surrounded her again, and she surreptitiously tried to breathe it in.

He smelled unbelievably good.

"But if I'm going to be your cover every time you see him, I think you should tell me what happened." His breath stirred the strands that had slipped out of her ponytail, tickling her ear.

"Later. I don't want him to hear me." Leaning forward, she tried to catch a glimpse of Darrell. The bastard.

"Exactly how much of a date do you think we need this to be?" Jonah's lips brushing across her earlobe as he whispered startled a gasp out of her—and even better, distracted her from looking for Darrell.

"Um...maybe we should go." Accepting Jonah's suggestion might end up being more than she had bargained for.

"Or maybe we should show him what he's missing." With one smooth motion, Jonah lifted her half into his lap so that her back rested against his broad, strong chest. Brushing her ponytail out of his way, he ran his mouth across the nape of her neck — a light, shivery touch that wiped all other thought from her mind.

A tremor ran through him as he sat back in the seat, pulling her even closer. He might be pretending to be her date, but LeeAnn could feel the very real evidence of his arousal against her thigh.

I shouldn't encourage him.

He's only in town because he wants to find a way to allow an oil company to tear up the land I love.

But it might be worth any trouble later if it gave her jerk ex even a moment of dismay to see her with someone else.

A wicked smile flashed across her face. "Okay. For show," she said, then turned in his arms to kiss him.

• • •

When their lips met, Jonah suddenly lost all sense of time. LeeAnn didn't hold back, throwing her entire body into kissing him, twisting around to better touch her mouth to his — a position he would have claimed was impossible for anyone else. She wiggled back to sit more firmly on his lap, and the sensation of her ass brushing against him made his breath catch in his chest.

Her tongue slipped into his mouth, and he wrapped his hands around her waist, deepening the kiss even further.

After a long moment, she pulled away and stared up at him with heavy-lidded eyes.

"Wow," she murmured.

He let his body respond for him—even the sound of her voice made his cock jump.

"Man of Steel," she whispered, then laughed, as if to herself.

"Hi, Lec." The voice came from the other side of the booth, and Jonah looked up from LeeAnn's face, which had gone perfectly still.

"Darrell." He almost wished she would follow it up with one of the expletives she'd been attaching to the man's name, but she didn't. Instead, she pressed her back against his chest, like an animal retreating from danger.

He could feel the rage rising in him again.

"I see your friend's here, too." Darrell Vincent—*man slut*, Jonah couldn't help adding—nodded at him.

LeeAnn's ex was leaning over their table a little too aggressively for Jonah's taste, pulling some subtle dominance act designed to intimidate LeeAnn and her companion while Jonah was seated.

It didn't take much to figure out the man was a bully, determined to make LeeAnn—and by extension, Jonah—uncomfortable. "Good to see you someplace so...public," Darrell said.

Is he truly that stupid? Apparently so.

Jonah lifted LeeAnn up and gently deposited her on the seat next to him. He swung his legs out of the booth and stood up, forcing Darrell to step back or risk getting kicked.

"Nice to officially meet you, Darrell," he said, reaching out to grasp the other's man hand in a not-quite-crushing grip. He stood at least three inches taller than the other man, and he again used his height to his advantage, moving into Darrell's space and looming over him.

Darrell took a step back and disentangled his hand. His new fiancée watched the exchange with cool, disinterested eyes.

She's not half the woman LeeAnn is. What's wrong with this douche?

Not that it mattered, as long as the douche left LeeAnn alone.

"Enjoy your dinner," Jonah said, nodding at Darrell's companion in a clear dismissal.

"You, too," the other man said, but he made no move back toward his own table, instead staring at Jonah and LeeAnn through narrowed eyes.

If I don't get out of here, I will end up hurting him.

"Actually, we were just leaving." Jonah flashed a smile in LeeAnn's direction. "We decided we have better things to do." He pulled a hundred-dollar bill out of his wallet and tossed it on the table. Another step into Vincent's space caused the man to step back again, allowing enough room for LeeAnn to exit the booth.

LeeAnn blinked several times, then snagged her purse. "Oh. Absolutely," she said, sliding out of her seat and running her fingers across Jonah's abdomen as she moved past him. "Much better things." She smirked at Darrell and waggled her fingers as they walked past. Jonah's arms hovered around her, clearly protecting her.

As Jonah ushered her to the door, he whispered into her ear, "Don't look back. It'll spoil a great exit line."

Outside the Wagon Wheel, LeeAnn let out a laugh that

he suspected would have been a whoop if they had been only slightly farther away from the diner. "Nicely done, Jonah Hamilton," she said. Her smile dimmed a bit. "Much better than last night."

Jonah smiled a little ruefully as they made their way down the sidewalk. "I wish I'd thought to grab our plates on the way out, though," he said.

"Come on," she said, tugging him across the street. "I know a great Mexican place. I'll buy you dinner. It's the least I can do."

"Only if you promise to make it free of any of your exes. I think I've used up all my manly prowess for the rest of the week."

Her eyes raked across him in a way that made him seriously consider actually skipping dinner. "Oh, I doubt that," she said. "I suspect you've got more manly prowess than you need."

Somehow, I'm not sure that's a compliment.

Shaking his head, he followed her through the streets of the Stockyards District.

Why does it matter what she thinks?

If he wasn't careful, he would end up leaving his heart here when he moved on to the next job.

Chapter Sixteen

Their days fell into a rhythm. Three days a week, after her morning class, she drove him to the ranch, where they spent the day searching through Gran's boxes, making their way through one outbuilding at a time. On the other days, he brought out his pickup and they loaded it with the things she had decided to donate to Goodwill or have hauled to the county dump. In the evenings, they went to dinner together after her class.

In between, LeeAnn did her best not to spend most of her time staring at him and daydreaming about the kisses they had shared.

For his part, Jonah seemed to ignore the chemistry she was certain she felt between them.

Then again, maybe he wasn't really interested in her, no matter what his body had suggested when she was sitting on his lap.

He certainly didn't mention the kisses again.

At the end of three weeks, they had cleared several outbuildings and a barn, with nothing to show for it but a growing collection of pictures of old magazines to send to his librarian friend—and on LeeAnn's part, a growing fascination with all things Jonah.

With that one exception at the party, where he had looked like he was about to actually beat Darrell to a pulp, he was smart, funny, nice—the type of man she had always admired.

Even if he was the enemy.

The kind of enemy she could learn to love?

She groaned aloud and unrolled her mat on the floor at the front of the mirrored room in the yoga studio. She needed this. Hours spent with Jonah only a few feet away had left her with something resembling a migraine headache.

It's not that he's beautiful and distracting.

Well, that's not all of it, anyway.

He was also determined to find proof that he was right—that Gran, or someone before her, had left the mineral rights to her ranch to someone else. That conviction rolled off him in waves, leaving her dizzy with…

Anger. Definitely anger.

Not desire.

Dropping down into a cross-legged lotus position, she pulled her feet up onto her thighs and touched her forefingers to her thumbs. Closing her eyes, she took in a deep breath, then gently blew it out, imagining that Jonah—and everything he did or said—went right out with the breath.

I am peaceful.

I am centered.

Om…

Calm settled over her shoulders, and she pulled it around herself like a warm fleece blanket.

Opening her eyes, she smiled beatifically and began greeting her students as they arrived, murmuring their names. This was the beginners' class, so she had people of all shapes and ages, ranging from high school students to senior citizens. Carlos Canas was the oldest in her class — he had been practicing for years before LeeAnn had even been born. She often asked him to demonstrate poses so she could point out specific elements to the class. He almost always arrived last, coming from volunteering at the local senior citizens' center.

He was also generally the only man in the class.

Most Texas men weren't really the yoga type.

"Hey, LeeAnn," Carlos said as he unrolled his own mat in front of hers.

She responded with a smile, then stood. "Time to get started, everyone," she said to the students, allowing the comfortable rhythm of the class to lengthen the cadence of her voice. "Roll your shoulders back, centered above your hips. Feet shoulder width apart, arms at your sides. Now close your eyes, and breathe."

As she closed her own eyes in demonstration, she heard a slight commotion. For a moment, she ignored it — although all her regulars were here, it wasn't exactly unusual for a newbie to show up a few minutes late. The other students would help the new arrival find a spot for her mat.

"And breathe in…and out."

The slight commotion had mostly died down, but an odd, expectant energy filled the room, blowing through the air around her.

What is that?

"Feel your feet rooted to the ground." She kept her voice slow and gentle, but the strange feeling continued to hover.

Cracking open one eyelid, she peeked at the room, then opened both eyes in surprise.

At the back of the room, towering over the women around him, stood Jonah, wearing soft gray sweatpants and a sleeveless T-shirt.

Her students glanced back and forth between their instructor and Jonah, and LeeAnn realized she had stopped speaking.

Jonah realized it at the same time and smirked. His navy blue eyes glinted at her.

Dammit. I am not peaceful. Not centered.

But he didn't need to see that.

Moving back into the routine, she took the class through their opening stretches.

Again and again, she found herself watching Jonah.

He moves like an athlete—light on his feet.

He stretched his arms high above his head, according to her instruction, then bent down toward his toes. He couldn't quite reach them.

Not terribly flexible, though.

Why is he here?

I wonder what he'd be like in bed?

She tried to shove the traitorous thought back down.

A hot blush flashed across her face, and she bent down to hide it as she took the class through the rest of the sun salutation. As they shifted into the standing poses, she began walking around the room, touching a student's back here, straightening a stance there.

I should help him. She sneaked a glance at him as he stood in the warrior one pose. His arms were in the correct position, but he needed to adjust his feet.

Stifling a sigh, she moved toward him.

I can do this. He's just another student.

Why does he get to me like this?

She moved around so she stood behind him. "What are you doing here?" she hissed.

"Yoga." His tone was bland, and he kept his gaze pointed toward the front of the room, but LeeAnn was certain she saw the corner of his mouth twitch.

Fine. He wanted to do yoga? She could arrange for that.

"Okay," she murmured, gently touching the undersides of his outstretched arms to lift them a little. She had planned to immediately bend over and readjust the placement of his feet. But as her fingertips brushed his bare skin, an electric shock jumped between them. She jerked her fingers back, curling them into fists, but it didn't stop the frisson of heat from running up her own arms. Startled, she glanced up at Jonah's face, in time to see a muscle in his cheek twitch.

He felt that, too.

She waited for some acknowledgment from him, but he didn't look at her, choosing instead to resettle himself into the warrior pose.

Okay, then. I can ignore it if he can.

Bending over, she tapped his back leg, making sure she didn't touch any bare skin this time. Thank God he was wearing sweats and not shorts.

"Turn this foot out, a little," she whispered, placing her foot beside his to demonstrate.

This time he glanced back at her, and she suddenly

became aware of how close they were. The heat of his body radiated out, warming the space between them. Pulling away, she glanced back one last time to make sure he had adjusted the pose.

His feet were perfectly aligned.

In fact, his feet were pretty much perfect.

Who has sexy feet?

Well, okay, probably Superman.

And apparently his cowboy alter ego.

Pay attention to the class, LeeAnn.

She moved them through the other warrior poses, then into triangle, a pose the class had been working on perfecting for the last two weeks.

"I know it seems like a simple pose," she said, "but remember, it's possible to make tiny changes and gain huge results. So let's keep working on creating the most beautiful triangles we can. Arms straight out, legs apart. Turn the front foot forward and your palms up. Shift your hip back, and slide your arm forward. Now, keeping your arms aligned, point the back one to the sky, and slide the bottom one toward the floor." She reached out and grabbed the blue foam block near her feet. "Remember, you can always balance on the block."

Once again, she stood and walked around the room.

This time, Jonah's foot placement was perfect.

He's a quick study.

Unlike many of the other people in the class full of beginner yoga students, he had opted not to use a block to steady himself, relying instead on the strength in his core to support him. As LeeAnn watched him, his shirt slipped up a little, baring the skin above the waistband of his sweats.

His skin stretched over the oblique muscle as it tensed with exertion.

I'm staring again.

"Everyone breathe," she intoned, as much a reminder to herself as it was to the class.

She moved back to the front of the room and resumed her demonstration of the pose. "Stretch up to the sky with one arm, down to the ground with other. Open your body to the side of the room," she said. "If you're comfortable here, then you might try turning your face to the sky." Several students—those who had been in her class for a while now—had actually already done so, and she was pleased to see their improved form.

Although she didn't want to admit it to herself, she was watching Jonah out of the corner of her eye to see if he felt steady enough in the position to add the extra balancing element of turning his head.

It didn't take long before he tried.

Okay. So he's not bad at yoga.

I wonder how long he can hold the pose.

It wasn't fair to the other students, she knew. But somehow, she couldn't help herself.

Not fair. Yeah, but it's not fair that he's so good at everything, either.

I know that the whole reason he's here is to mess with me. I'm sure of it.

So let's see how long he lasts.

"Okay," she said. "Remember, everyone, listen to your body. We are going to hold this pose for as long as you feel comfortable. When you're ready, drop down into child's pose by bringing your arms up and stepping your feet together. Then kneel down, place your forehead on the mat, and stretch your arms out in front of you." Quickly, she demonstrated. "Anytime you like, you can bring your arms back alongside your legs, palms up, and rest."

About half the class followed her lead almost immediately. The other half, including Jonah, opted to stay in triangle, and LeeAnn rose up to resume the pose, as well.

One. Two. Three. She began counting the seconds in her head.

After a minute, half of the remaining students stepped out of the pose.

But not Jonah.

From her position at the front of the room, LeeAnn could see sweat begin to bead on his forehead.

One hundred and thirty-eight. Thirty-nine. Forty.

"Remember to breathe," she instructed the class. "In and out."

This is my territory.

You won't win.

One hundred seventy-five. Seventy-six.

• • •

Jonah blinked as a bead of sweat trickled down his forehead and into his eye.

He had come to the class to see LeeAnn in a different setting. In his experience, seeing someone at work could tell him a lot about how to deal with them. He needed more information about LeeAnn. Ever since that second kiss, she had seemed more distant, cooler.

He wanted to change that, if only because they still had

several buildings to go through before they finished their search through her gran's paperwork.

Mineral rights. That's why you're hanging out in her yoga studio.

Yeah, right.

You're an idiot, Hamilton.

This wasn't the first time he'd been in a yoga class—not exactly, anyway. A college girlfriend had dragged him to a few sessions, so he understood the basic concept. He hadn't ever been in one like this, though. Somehow, he hadn't ever considered yoga an endurance sport.

But this pose was about to kill him.

Time to drop into—what had she called it? Child's pose.

As he opened his eyes, though, he caught a glimpse of her staring at him, her own gray eyes narrowed as her gaze bored into him, followed almost instantly by a shock of realization.

She's doing this because of me.

He glanced around, seeing the rest of the students begin to sit up. They glanced nervously at their instructor, as if waiting for her to speak.

Oh. It's on.

He closed his eyes and settled back into the pose, ignoring the burn of the muscles along his side.

I've dealt with worse than this.

A muscle in his jaw jumped, and he focused on forcing it to relax. What was that thing the yoga teacher in college had said?

Oh, yeah.

Om...

See? It was easy.

Except that now his neck was beginning to cramp up. And his arm, the one pointing up into the air, had started to go numb.

Still, he couldn't let her win.

On some level, he knew he shouldn't care who won, shouldn't even see it as a competition. He couldn't seem to help himself.

Finally, though, he had to acknowledge that at least in this arena, he might have to admit defeat.

I am too old for this. And far too mature.

Suddenly, Jonah didn't care whether he won or not. Not against her.

Now, I need to get out of this damn pose.

Opening his eyes, he began to exert his stiffened muscles to raise up, to bring his arms level. A gentle touch at his waist and under one arm guided him up, and he realized that LeeAnn was standing behind him.

"Excellent work," she said, smiling at him. Some sort of acknowledgment passed between them, and then she was walking away, threading her way through the mats and talking to the class again. "Great job, everyone. Now let's move on to today's balance pose."

What was that, exactly?

It was important. I'm sure of it.

He had originally come to the class to attempt to gain some insight into this strange, compelling woman. So how did this oddly competitive moment fit into the overall picture he was building up of her?

It doesn't. Not really. That was your cutthroat nature showing itself, Hamilton.

And yet she had joined in the silent war.

Yoga as a nervous habit.

Yoga as a competitive sport.

A ranch that was falling apart.

A recent breakup with a man who clearly didn't recognize what he'd had.

A woman who had kissed him on impulse, drawing out of him the strongest reaction he'd had to anyone in a long time.

She ran hot and cold.

Mostly hot.

Shaking his head, he stretched his aching arms out in front of him, following her instructions as she led the class into what he recognized as the odd crane stance she'd been practicing in the store the first time he'd seen her there.

He was looking forward to continuing to work with her—to learning more about the kind of woman who was willing to test his limits.

Maybe all of my limits.

An unwilling smile crept across his face.

Chapter Seventeen

He walked toward the corral, the path familiar after weeks of treading it every weekday morning. As usual, he eyed the fences as he walked—particularly the barbed-wire fence that marked the property's outer boundary. Parts of it were sagging, and some of the fence posts had fallen down altogether.

Frowning, he paused by one of the downed posts, toeing it with one boot. It wouldn't be that hard to fix. Not with the right equipment.

A plan began forming in his mind.

After he'd said hello to the horse, he headed back to the house. As usual, LeeAnn was already up and about, a cup of hot tea in her hand. It didn't matter what time he arrived, she was always awake and moving.

He, on the other hand, couldn't function until he'd had at least two cups of strong black coffee.

"Good morning," she warbled.

"Hey," he said. "Would it be okay with you if I rode Blackie sometime? It's been too long since I've been riding."

"Sure," she said. "We usually go out first thing in the morning, but he could use more exercise."

First thing in the morning? Wasn't *this* first thing in the morning?

"Thanks," he said.

"No problem. The gear's in the stable—the one up by the house, not the shelter out by the pastures." She waved toward the appropriate building.

He nodded. "I saw it on the first day."

As they headed into the house, he felt particularly pleased with himself, even though he knew he probably shouldn't.

It's not my fault she can't take care of her property.

But he was going to do something about it, anyway.

• • •

Hours later, LeeAnn lifted a box off the top of the dwindling stack in the attic. "Are we doing dinner tonight after my class?" she asked as she swung it to the floor. "If so, I want to stop by Cowbelles to talk to Kylie for a minute."

"You missing the place?" Jonah's tone was teasing.

Keep it professional, she admonished herself, as she had been doing for days on end—but it was difficult when every glance made her want to crawl into his lap, despite all the reasons she knew she shouldn't.

Like the fact that he's still trying to find a way to allow his company to start drilling.

But even if the job they were doing appalled her,

focusing on it kept her from going insane with all the not touching going on.

"Yeah, but mostly I wanted to invite them to join us. I haven't seen either of them much since they got back." Her voice was distracted as she opened the box, pulled out a faded blue and white quilt, and stared at it. "I think Gran may have made this," she said. "Or maybe her mother? I can't believe it was shoved in a box and put away." Moving over to the doorway, she added it to the growing pile of things she planned to keep.

"So how early do we need to go?" He glanced at his watch. "If you want to go by the store, we should probably knock off in an hour or two."

Checking her own watch, LeeAnn nodded. "Definitely. I need a shower before we go into town. I don't want to scare off my yoga students, coming into class all stinky and disgusting."

"I thought you yogi types covered stinky with some kind of perfumey oil." His grin took any sting out of the words.

LeeAnn snorted, then covered her mouth and nose, embarrassed. "Patchouli? Gran always said it reminded her of the smell of the weeds she pulled out of the garden every spring. The one time I came home wearing it, she sent me straight upstairs to take a shower."

"I think I might have liked your gran." His blue eyes sparkled at her.

"She would have liked you, too." She considered that for a moment, then revised her comment. "At least, until she figured out that you were here to help people drill on her land. Then she would have kicked you out on your ass."

Now it was his turn to snort. "I might have liked her

even more for trying." He dropped a stack of books back into a box. "Since I don't have any patchouli, either, maybe I could borrow your shower before we go?"

The thought of him in her shower sent a bolt of pure sensation through her, bringing every nerve alive.

"Sure." She even managed to keep her voice from sounding too strangled.

Oh, no.

She fought to keep from moaning aloud—but inside, she wailed.

What have I done?

I can't—Can. Not.—fall for him. He's wrong for me in every way.

Besides, I know exactly what I want in a relationship.

She began listing her boyfriend qualifications—the same list she'd had for three years.

I want someone smart. Preferably into yoga.

He has to be a vegetarian—we have to agree on the basic value of life or we can't possibly be together.

He needs to be kind, and he has to love animals.

Well, okay. So Jonah fit those last two. He didn't fit the rest of the list.

She had already tried the opposites-attract route, and it just didn't work. Darrell hadn't fit her qualifications, either, and look what had happened with him.

"Did you growl?" Jonah asked, looking up from the piece of paper he'd plucked out of a magazine.

"What? No. Of course not." LeeAnn blew an errant hair out of her eyes. "What's that? Did you find something?"

"Not really," he said. "Looks like a recipe of some sort."

"What for?" She held her hand out.

"Buttermilk pie." Leaning over, he passed the paper to her. "One of my favorites."

"Mine, too," she said.

"Yeah?" Going back to flipping through the magazine pages, he smiled. "I lived in Louisiana for a year when I first started working for Natural Shale—I did some training in the Gulf of Mexico. I was stunned when I discovered I couldn't get buttermilk pie at any of the restaurants there."

"Oh, the horror." Faking a gasp, LeeAnn put her hand over her heart.

"You have no idea." Jonah grinned up at her, his dimples out in full force. "They actually think that bread pudding is a viable dessert."

"Bread pudding does come with rum sauce," LeeAnn said, setting the recipe on top of a small pile of papers she had gathered to take back to the house. It was in her grandmother's handwriting—a tiny treasure that she hadn't known existed.

At least she was managing to save some important things.

Just not my heart.

"The rum is pretty much the only thing that makes the stuff edible." Jonah's words brought LeeAnn's attention back to the discussion of desserts.

After a moment of silence, LeeAnn and Jonah sighed, in unison. Then they looked at each other and burst into startled laughter.

"So was it the bread pudding that sent you running back to Texas?" LeeAnn asked.

"Oh, no. It was my father." Jonah's derisive snort surprised her—she hadn't expected their conversation to turn dark. She waited silently to see if he would elaborate.

"I was fresh out of college, and Natural Shale was my first job. They were going to be sending me all over the country to learn the business from the ground up." He picked up a tiny piece of paper debris from the floor and rolled it between his thumb and forefinger.

"As a landman?"

"No. I was planning to go back to school to become a petrochemical engineer—the science aspect of the job really drew me." His mouth twisted up as he shook his head. "But then Dad lost his job—again. My kid sister was still in high school, and I was the only one in the family who could help. He and Mom divorced when I was young, so she sure wasn't going to step in."

"So you stayed in your job." She had meant it to be a question, but it hadn't come out that way.

"Yep." He flicked the miniscule paper ball he'd been worrying between his fingers away with his thumb. "Been supporting him ever since, on and off. I will *never* be a burden to my family."

The vehemence of his words took her by surprise.

Even Jonah seemed startled by the intensity with which he spoke, because he blinked once, then immediately tried to lighten the mood. "Okay," he said, stretching his arms out in front of him. "That's it. I clearly need a break. And I'm guessing you do, too." He placed one hand on the ground and shoved himself to his feet, his boots making thumping noises on the floor.

"Yes, of course." LeeAnn worked to match his tone. "If I had any buttermilk pie, I'd say we needed that, too."

"At this point," Jonah replied, "I'd settle for bread pudding." He motioned for her to head down the stairs in front of him.

And he's a gentleman, too. I am in such deep trouble.

"Well, I don't have either one," she said.

"Then I think it's time for that shower we discussed earlier." Jonah's voice floated down the stairs after her, and when she turned to look back, he was watching her with a devilish grin. "Or those showers, I should say."

The thought of showering with Jonah in the old claw-foot tub in her guest bathroom sent chills running up and down her spine.

Damn the man for knowing how to get to her.

"R-right," she managed to stammer out.

"Great—I've got clothes in the truck." At the landing, she stepped aside, and he jogged down the rest of the stairs.

Clothes in the truck?

Had he planned this?

No. Of course he hadn't. He worked for an oil company. He probably kept a change of clothes in his truck in case he needed them.

In case he got covered in oil, for example.

Or evil.

Right, LeeAnn. He keeps a change of clothes in his truck in case he gets soaked in evil.

She waited long enough for him to return so she could point him toward the shower. "Back in fifteen," she said.

His smirk suggested he didn't believe her.

Yeah, well. He'll see soon enough.

Now if only she could quit thinking about his broad shoulders and bare chest, slick with soap, water running down his flat stomach…

Quit it.

Shaking her head, she shut herself into her bathroom.

Thank God we're inviting Kylie and Cole to go with us.

. . .

The interior of the small shop was cool. Jonah wandered through the sparkling displays of Texas-themed merchandise—much of it covered in sequins and rhinestones—as LeeAnn headed toward the back of the store, calling out as she went. "Kylie?"

"Oh, hey, Lee." Kylie came out of the back, smoothing down her dress. Her light brown hair was mussed, and her lips were slightly swollen. Glancing back at the stockroom, the store owner said, "I wasn't expecting you."

With a grin, LeeAnn replied, "Apparently." She raised her voice. "Cole? You there?"

The country singer stepped through the door, tucking his white dress shirt into his jeans. He drew LeeAnn into a hug. "Good to see you," he said.

"Glad you're home," LeeAnn said. "I'm headed to class in a minute, but I thought I'd see if y'all wanted to join us for dinner tonight." She turned to include Jonah in the conversation. "Cole, this is Jonah Hamilton. He's"—she paused, almost imperceptibly—"helping me sort through some of Gran's old paperwork."

"That must be a monster of a job." Kylie had clearly seen the outbuildings at some point.

Dinner with his favorite country music star hadn't been in Jonah's plans, but maybe getting to know her friends could also help him figure LeeAnn out.

And honestly, anything sounds better than another class

in competitive yoga.

"We're planning to hit the new diner after LeeAnn's class. Want to meet us there?" he said, seconding the invitation.

The couple glanced at one another, clearly communicating without words. Watching their easy rapport sent a twinge through him. Was that something he would ever experience?

Not if it means someone else might have to be responsible for me someday.

"Thanks, man," said Cole. "We'd love to." He paused, turning to his girlfriend. "Unless you had something else planned?"

A blush tinted Kylie's cheeks, causing the light dusting of freckles across her nose to stand out. She was pretty, in a slightly too curvy kind of way. Nothing like LeeAnn, though, with her long legs and strong, toned body.

"I've been wanting to try out the new place. We'll be there," Kylie said, and she and Cole walked them to the door.

"I'll walk to the studio from here," LeeAnn said as they stepped out onto the sidewalk. "I'll be done a little after seven."

He had been half tempted to figure out a way to watch while she taught her class tonight.

That wasn't creepy, was it?

"Sure," he said aloud, watching her long, steady stride as she moved away from him.

Only an hour and a half until he saw her again. Why did it suddenly seem like much longer?

Chapter Eighteen

Jonah leaned back against the leather booth, watching Lee-Ann as she laughed at Cole's story about his determination to win Kylie back after a yearlong separation. The waitress had removed their plates—the buttermilk pie had been as good as he had hoped—and replaced them with coffee cups for everyone but LeeAnn, who had ordered a cup of hot tea.

"And then," Cole was saying, "I figured out that Kylie had been going all over town, ripping down my concert posters."

With a shriek, Kylie slapped at the country star's shoulder. "I did not. I only took down the ones by my store. Anyway"—she turned to face Jonah—"he deserved it. Every single time I walked out my door, there his picture was, staring at me."

"But she had all his merchandise in the store," LeeAnn interjected, "so it's not like she wasn't seeing his face on a daily basis." She paused to aim a mock glare at her friend.

"Not that she ever told anyone that she even knew him."

Kylie's own face turned a bright shade of pink, and she shook her head. "It was no one else's business."

Slipping his arm around his blushing girlfriend's shoulder, Cole hugged her against him as he turned to Jonah. "So, how did you two hook up?" he asked, nodding his head to include LeeAnn in the question.

"We're not…" LeeAnn stammered at the same moment that Jonah said, "We're just working together."

"Oh," said Cole, surprised. "So did you hire Jonah to help you clear out your grandmother's outbuildings?"

"Actually," Jonah interjected smoothly, while LeeAnn struggled to find an answer, "it was the other way around. I'm paying her to help me look for anything about the mineral rights to her land."

Beside him, LeeAnn tensed, as if expecting a blow. Determined not to be the one to deliver it, even with words, Jonah did his best to keep his tone light. "We have different goals. I'm hoping we find something, LeeAnn's hoping we don't. So far, she's winning."

LeeAnn rolled her shoulders back, a move he now recognized as the first step in her yoga-as-nervous-habit routine.

Any minute now, she'll start breathing deeply.

But before anyone could respond, a girl, probably fifteen or sixteen, approached the table and asked, her voice shaking a bit, if she could have Cole's autograph.

Jonah was glad for the distraction. The last thing he had wanted to do tonight was send LeeAnn into a fit of yoga.

If she tries to stand on her head, I'll hurt someone.

The thought surprised him—but as he glanced over at

the woman beside him, he felt every protective instinct he owned rearing up, demanding that he keep her safe, at all costs.

Even if it means giving up the chance to find the drilling rights to her land?

The answer came to him, clear and strong. *Yes. Even then.*

Was there any way for both of them to win? He pushed the question aside to be examined later—when he wasn't surrounded by LeeAnn and her friends, laughing and talking, drawing him into their world, so different from his usual life of hotel rooms, library searches, and land surveys, his lonely dinners only sometimes punctuated by the company of oil-field hands and their managers. He kept an apartment out in Midland, near the company's headquarters, but unless his work took him that way, he rarely used it other than as a place to store his things, such as they were. It was almost as sterile as the hotel rooms he frequented.

Nothing like LeeAnn's old farmhouse, warm and inviting, even with its strangely packed attic and old-fashioned furniture.

When Cole finished talking to the fan, dismissing her with a smile as she clutched her newly autographed paper to her chest and returned to her family's table, Jonah leaned toward the other man. "How do you two deal with the whole being on the road issue?" he asked.

Kylie and Cole exchanged a sidelong glance, and for a moment, Jonah feared that he might have given away the direction of his thoughts. But Kylie's answer was straightforward. "Right now," she said, "we're doing two weeks on, four weeks off. LeeAnn covers the store for me when I'm gone."

"But I'm finishing up this tour soon," Cole said, "and then I'll be back here."

"That's right," Jonah said. "You bought a recording studio here recently, didn't you?"

Cole nodded. "I'm hoping to draw some other artists here, too, maybe do some collaboration."

As the conversation shifted to Cole's plans for a new record label of his own, LeeAnn's tight posture relaxed, and Jonah let his thoughts drift a bit—but again and again, he found himself returning to the same question.

What am I going to do next?

• • •

That went well, LeeAnn thought as she waved at Cole and Kylie, who headed in the opposite direction, back toward Cowbelles.

She was glad her friend had reunited with Cole—he clearly adored Kylie, and it had been a long time since LeeAnn had seen her so happy.

With a slight sigh, she turned and met Jonah's gaze as he watched her intently.

"I like your friends," he said. The comment itself was mild enough, but his tone was especially intense, as if he meant her to understand something more.

Quit reading into things, LeeAnn.

"I do, too," she said, working to ignore any possible undertones to their conversation. He fell into step beside her as she began walking down the sidewalk toward TexZen, where she had left her car, parked right next to his truck.

They walked in companionable silence for a long

moment, until LeeAnn said, "I don't have a class tomorrow morning."

"No problem," Jonah replied. "I wanted to bring the truck out anyway, to help haul away some of things you've decided to trash." A tiny smile played around his lips, his dimples flashing in and out almost too quickly to notice.

LeeAnn almost asked what he was thinking but decided it might be wiser to contain her curiosity. She was already far too invested in him.

The less I know about Jonah Hamilton, the better.

Somehow, the thought rang hollow.

When they turned to enter the yoga studio's parking lot, Jonah's hand hovered close to the small of her back, as if to direct her.

Or maybe to protect me?

LeeAnn shook the thought away, hiding the motion as she dug through her purse for her key fob. The silver Prius beeped and the headlights flashed in the dark. Other than a second hybrid—a bright blue Ford Focus that belonged to Angie, the studio's owner—her car and his truck were the only vehicles in the lot. The red-bricked streets were quiet, most of the area's stores having shut down for the night. She could hear the faint music coming from a bar a street or two over, but nothing stirred any closer. Suddenly, she felt glad for Jonah's protective presence.

Moving into the space between the Prius and the Chevrolet truck—1956 with a chrome bumper, she remembered with a smile—LeeAnn turned to say good-bye to Jonah, and was startled to find him standing right behind her.

Once she realized he was there, she couldn't imagine how she had missed his presence before. Electricity practically jumped between them as she tilted her head back to look up at him.

Jonah tilted his Stetson back on his head and leaned closer, then reached up and brushed one work-callused thumb across her bottom lip. Her breath caught in her chest, and she froze, uncertain what to do next.

"This could work," he whispered, so quietly that she couldn't tell if it was meant for her or not.

She stared up, mesmerized first by his full lips and then by his navy blue eyes, gazing intently at her, as if he meant to read her every thought with his eyes alone.

He's going to kiss me again.

She was sure of it.

Without an audience—for no reason other than...he wants to?

For a long moment, she stood perfectly still, waiting, not certain what she wanted him to do even as every cell of her body urged her toward him.

Then he blinked, and the spell was broken.

Taking a deep breath and blowing it back out as he stood up straight, Jonah dropped his hands gently onto her shoulders. "I'll see you tomorrow, okay?" he said, then reached around her to open the Prius's door.

LeeAnn's hands were still shaking as she started the car and pulled out of the parking lot.

What did he mean when he said this could work?

Us?

Chapter Nineteen

Closing out her morning practice the next day with a brief meditation, LeeAnn worked to ignore the excitement that fluttered through her stomach at the thought of Jonah showing up for another day of sorting through Gran's things.

She couldn't, however, ignore the fact that the excitement had nothing to do with searching the seemingly endless boxes of papers—and everything to do with Jonah.

No matter how hard she tried, she couldn't convince herself that she hadn't fallen for the man.

But I can at least keep him from figuring it out.

I can protect myself that way—because falling in love with someone like him is bound to end in heartache.

Anyway, he's only here because he wants to destroy my property.

My land.

My peace of mind.

She huffed a sigh. So much for meditation.

The second part of her morning was bound to cheer her up, though—saddling Blackie always made her smile. In fact, merely pulling on her jeans and boots brought a smile to her face.

But when she got to the barn, the saddle, saddle pad, and bridle were all missing.

Jonah must have decided to ride today.

That shouldn't have made her smile, but it did. It also made her want to see her favorite boy and his new friend—*Blackie*, she clarified. Blackie was her favorite boy.

Oh, God. I've got it bad. I wish I couldn't wait for us to be done with this search. Truth be told, though, I want it to drag out.

And she had to tell the truth—to herself, anyway, even if not to him.

The morning air still carried a slight chill, though the sun was beginning to burn away some of the dew that coated the short native grass lining the sides of the path down to the pastures. LeeAnn whistled a little as she made her way toward the paddock, half expecting to see Jonah and Blackie riding through the pastures.

They weren't there.

She frowned a little, her jaunty step slowing as she turned a complete circle, scanning for them.

It's not like I specified that he should stay in the pasture. Or on my property, for that matter.

Surely he hadn't taken Blackie off the ranch.

She drew in a deep breath, counting to herself, and blew it back out.

This is no big deal. I simply need to get to higher ground.

Without thinking, she turned toward the highest hill

on the property. She knew the land like she knew her own heart—and she could see everything from that point. At the top of the incline, she once again did a slow turn, gazing out across the ranch as she searched for her horse and the man riding him.

There—on the far eastern edge of the property, she could barely see him. She shaded her eyes against the glare of the rising sun. What was he doing? It looked like he had some sort of equipment. Like he was setting it up…

"Oh, no," she breathed aloud, then cursed. "He's already started surveying for the oil company." Heading down the hill, she continued muttering to herself. "That lousy, lying, cheating, thieving…"

At the bottom of the slope, she broke into a run, her boots slipping in the wet grass.

When she reached the house, she threw open the door. "Keys. Where are my keys?" Scrabbling through the bowl on the entryway table, she finally located them. Slamming the door behind her, she stomped down the porch steps toward her car, still grumbling under her breath.

The Prius wasn't really made for driving across the ranch—in fact, until recently, she'd still had her gran's beat-up old pickup. But it had finally died for good, so she had traded it in. She missed it now as she bumped across the east field. Before her grandfather had died, they'd had cattle in this field, so at least it had been cleared at some point.

The thought caused her to slow down. She couldn't afford to break an axle—or whatever it was that cars had these days—just because some jerk had stolen her horse in an attempt to rape her land.

Oh, yes. Rape. Pillage. Defile. Destroy.

It doesn't matter what he calls it. That's what it really is. I bet his company plans to…to frack it.

Never mind that she didn't really know what fracking was. She knew it was something terrible that oil companies did to the land in order to get oil. And that it had caused earthquakes all along the Permian Basin.

Earthquakes.

In Texas.

That slimy prick is going to cause an earthquake on my ranch.

She could feel a hot rage welling up in her throat, choking her, and as she came over a slight rise in the land, almost the only thing that kept her from stepping on the gas and running right over the lying ass-hat was the fact that her beloved horse stood next to him.

Never, in a million years, would she do anything to hurt Blackie.

She stepped on the brake, and the Prius swung in a wide arc before coming to a stop.

Wait. I wouldn't do anything to hurt anyone.

I won't even eat meat.

What is wrong with me?

In that final skid, her car had ended up turned sideways rather than facing Jonah, so through the windshield, all she saw in front of her was the wide expanse of land that she had inherited from her gran, and in the distance, the house, the barn, and all the outbuildings, slowly falling in on themselves.

What had she been thinking?

She'd been thinking of the days that she had "helped" her grandfather fix that recalcitrant old tractor, handing him tools and solemnly promising not to tell Gran when he cursed in front of her.

Hours spent cooking in the kitchen with Gran—making those buttermilk pies so often that she didn't even need the recipe she and Jonah had found.

The long nights after her parents' deaths, when Gran would come into her bedroom and rock her, the two of them clinging to one another in their shared grief.

The first time she'd been able to ride Blackie, when he was finally filled out enough so his ribs didn't show and his coat had turned a sleek, glossy black.

She'd been thinking of everything she'd had.

Everything she'd lost.

For years, she had been hanging on to the ranch with everything she had inside, clawing at the world to keep from having to sell off acres or mortgage the land—to keep the promise she had made to her gran, whose own parents' experiences during the Great Depression had left a generations-long horror of allowing banks too much access to the land they held.

She was the only person she could trust to take care of the land Gran had left her. No one else cared enough.

For the first time ever, that made her feel lonely instead of strong.

Tears welled up in her eyes, and she dropped her head onto her hands on the steering wheel. She hadn't cried since Darrell had called to break up with her over a month ago, but now deep, heaving sobs racked her body.

The sharp rap at the window startled her. She'd been so lost in her own misery that for a moment, she'd completely forgotten Jonah and his treachery.

His face loomed close, separated from her by only the

thin glass.

Moments ago, she had been prepared to run him down for betraying her trust. Now, she couldn't even bring herself to care enough to even look up at him.

"LeeAnn?" His voice echoed through the window, worry coloring his tone. "Are you okay? What happened?"

When she didn't answer, he pulled at the handle. "Open the door. Please. I need to know you're okay."

Finally, she dragged her head up from its resting spot on the steering wheel.

What did it matter if he had already started surveying?

If they didn't find anything proving that she had the right to tell Natural Shale to take a hike, then the company would bring in its lawyers. She couldn't compete with that. She didn't have the money. And right now, she didn't have the heart.

Turning her tearstained face toward the window, she dragged her eyes up to his as she unlocked the door.

"What is it?" Jonah asked, pulling open the car door and leaning in. "Are you okay?" He reached past her and unbuckled the seat belt, then took her hands in his and turned her to face him as he knelt down next to the car.

She looked down into his eyes for a moment, then turned her head to stare blankly out the window.

It was like he was two people. How could he be so kind in one moment, then turn around and callously undermine everything he knew she cared about?

"Talk to me, LeeAnn. Please tell me what's going on." He squeezed her hands, trying to pull her attention back to him.

Blackie stood next to the fence, tethered to a post,

placidly grazing as far as the line would reach. The car slewing sideways hadn't even fazed him.

As she stared at the fence outside the windshield, the tools Jonah had been using came into focus.

She hadn't realized that surveyors used wire to do their jobs.

Wait. Is that a post-hole digger?

And that fence post Blackie was tethered to looked... odd. One side was darker than the other. As if it had been lying on the ground for some time and had only recently been brought upright again.

The realization hit her hard.

Jonah hadn't been surveying her land at all. He had been riding her fence, fixing it as he went.

Hot embarrassment threaded its way through her entire body, starting in her stomach and twisting into her arms and legs, up to her face, where it burned bright red.

Finally, she looked at Jonah, whose worried gaze still centered on her eyes.

"Well, this is embarrassing," she said, and exploded in hysterical laughter.

• • •

For a moment, Jonah thought that LeeAnn was sobbing. But then she raised her eyes to his, and he realized that although she was crying, they were tears of laughter.

She gasped, trying to speak. "I thought that you"—more insane giggles—"I thought that you were surveying." The last word came out in a howl, followed by more wild laughter.

"No." A broad sweep of his arm served to take in the fence, the horse, the tools he'd brought along. "I saw some spots that needed work," he said, shrugging. "I thought I'd ride the fences and see what I could fix."

A sudden, uncomfortable twist in his stomach suggested that perhaps he hadn't fully considered the possible implications of his actions. Riding the fences certainly implied a level of…if not ownership, at least possessiveness…that LeeAnn might not appreciate—at least not as much as he had hoped, on some subliminal level, that she would appreciate having the fences fixed.

In his job—and in his private life, for that matter—he was used to considering actions, not motivations. Or at least, not his own motivations. He studied clients' needs, considered their motivations, desires—all in an attempt to make a drilling lease offer that would satisfy both Natural Shale and the landowners.

So what had happened here?

What was I thinking?

Her giggles finally died out, and he feared she might be considering some of the same implications. "You were fixing the fence?" she finally asked.

Still working to sift through his own motivations, he simply nodded.

"Why?" Her mouth tightened into a small bow, and the sudden urge to kiss it until it softened again hit him so hard he felt a little dizzy. Why, indeed?

Why would a man with absolutely no connection to the ranch decide to ride the fences?

Unless he wanted to prove something.

Or show something.

Oh, shit.

He'd done it. He'd gone and fallen for the hippie yoga chick. Not some kind of opposites-attract lust. That he knew how to handle: get the girl in bed, have fun, go home.

But this? This is something different.

The long silence led LeeAnn to prompt him again. "So?"

He shrugged. "I needed to get outside for a while." With a jerk of his chin, he indicated the rest of the ranch, with its dilapidated outbuildings full of dusty boxes.

Flicking her narrowed gaze from Jonah, to the fence, to the horse, to the rest of the ranch, and back again, LeeAnn sat back in the seat, still clutching the top of the steering wheel. "Huh." Closing her eyes and shaking her head, she banged her forehead against the backs of her hands several times, finally coming to rest with her face pressed against them.

A flash of alarm shot through him as he realized that her shoulders were shaking. Was she crying again?

"LeeAnn?" he asked, working to keep the worry he felt from leaking into his tone.

But when she lifted her face from her hands, he realized that the tears streaming down her face were from laughter. She wiped her palms across her eyes, then her fingertips, clearing away the tears as she shook her head. "I'm sorry. I think I might be a little bit insane."

He wanted to reassure her that she wasn't—but to be honest, he wasn't entirely certain of her sanity, himself. It didn't make sense that she wouldn't take the company's offer—an offer that would leave her with enough money to pay her taxes and hire real help to fix the fences, repair the outbuildings, and paint the house.

If she's insane, what does it say about me that I'm attracted to her?

Because that's all it could be. A crazy attraction.

Fine—so the pull he felt toward her seemed to tug at some deep part of himself, some newly discovered sense of…what? Protectiveness?

Yeah. That was it.

He hadn't fallen for her—that would mean *he* was the crazy one.

LeeAnn Walker was a neo-hippie part-time yoga instructor with a ranch that was falling apart and not enough sense to take the one offer that would solve all her problems.

She was a vegetarian. Her Prius sported a MEAT IS MURDER bumper sticker.

She cuts fake nuts off pickup trucks, for Chrissakes.

Clearly, she needed protection—from herself, if nothing else.

That was why he was out here first thing in the morning, working a fence that wasn't his job.

Having worked out an explanation for his own actions—and more importantly, for the way her every motion pulled at him—Jonah nodded firmly. "I'm almost finished here," he said. "Let's go back down to the house and see if we can go through the last of the boxes today." Rapping once on the hood for emphasis, he stepped back, ignoring the urge to brush away the one glittering tear that remained suspended on LeeAnn's flushed cheek.

With a nod, LeeAnn put the Prius into reverse. "I'll see you down there," she said.

Jonah lifted one hand and waved, forcing himself to turn toward the fence rather than watch her drive away.

The silence left in the wake of the retreating car was broken only by Blackie, snuffling through the grass at the limits of his tether. When Jonah stepped up beside him, the gelding nuzzled his pockets, searching for treats. Jonah pulled out the last of the sugar cubes he'd secreted there and held them out on his palm, where Blackie delicately lipped them up as Jonah stroked his mane.

Staring blindly at the fence in front of him as he thumped his palm against the horse's neck, Jonah said companionably, "Oh, yeah, boy. That's it. I'm screwed."

Chapter Twenty

Even after a full day of searching through reams of paper, then lugging out boxes of trash and heaving them into the back of Jonah's pickup to haul away, LeeAnn hadn't slept well—despite being utterly exhausted when she fell into bed that night. Instead, she tossed and turned, unable to quit thinking about Jonah.

She spent the entire next morning thinking about him, too—about everything that had happened in the weeks since she had met him.

Jonah, kissing her in the Wagon Wheel—twice—to help her deal with Darrell.

Cutting mesquite wood for a party and never complaining, even when he got hurt.

Standing up to Darrell at the party.

Fitting in perfectly with Kylie and Cole.

Almost kissing her in the TexZen Yoga Studio parking lot.

Fixing her fence.

Spending hour upon hour sorting through piles of old junk, stopping to hand her anything she might find valuable, stepping in to help her lift the heavy boxes, laughing with her at the funny images in old magazines.

Paying her to do a job that she might have had to do anyway, if the Natural Shale lawyers had stepped in.

Was he right? Could this work—this thing between them that they had never mentioned, but that she was certain they both felt? Could she come to terms with what he did for a living? Or did their differences outweigh their similarities?

Does it really matter, given how much I want him?

At the moment, Jonah was bending over as he took another picture to send to his librarian friend. LeeAnn couldn't take her eyes off him. When he turned to say something to her, he caught her staring at him.

For once, she didn't glance away, though she could feel her cheeks heating up as he regarded her steadily.

Jonah didn't break eye contact, either. Instead, he took a purposeful stride toward her, and her breath caught in her throat.

Stopping in front of her, he brushed a strand of hair off her cheek. "You keep looking at me like that, and I'm going to take it as an invitation," he said quietly.

"Maybe you should," she whispered.

He closed his eyes briefly.

Was that the wrong thing to say?

She had enough time to begin worrying when he spoke again, relieving her anxiety.

"Tell you what. I'm going to go downstairs and take a shower." His voice sounded deep and strained, and his gaze was hot on her mouth. "You take a minute to be sure." He took her chin in his hand and grazed his mouth across hers. "And if you're absolutely certain, you can join me there."

He took a step back, and then, with a scorching glance back at her, he headed down the stairs.

LeeAnn hesitated outside the bathroom door.

If she opened it, there would be no turning back.

Could she take what he had to offer—everything his kisses had promised—knowing that it was only temporary?

Then again, life was only temporary, nothing permanent enough to count on forever.

Darrell Dumbass Liar Vincent had taught her that.

Right?

The memory of Sami telling her she didn't trust anyone twisted in her chest. Had she really chosen Darrell because she knew, on some level, that he would hurt her?

Am I doing it again?

She shoved the thought away. Anyway, it didn't matter. If everything was temporary, she might as well take what she could, while she could. Closing her eyes, she used a few deep breaths to calm her mind.

This time, she would let her body take the lead.

She opened the door and stepped inside.

• • •

A smile flitted across Jonah's face when he heard the door begin to open, but by the time LeeAnn moved into the small space, his face was solemn. Her gray eyes were wide, and she very carefully looked at nothing but his eyes, even though he hadn't taken off anything other than his shirt. He leaned back against the sink, his hands propping him up as he waited to see what she would do next.

"Hey," she finally said, her voice low.

"Hey," he replied, matching her tone. "Are you planning to wear that in the shower?" he asked, nodding toward her dusty clothes.

Without a word, she drew her T-shirt up over her head and tossed it in a corner, then stepped out of her jeans. There was nothing overtly seductive about the moves—they were straightforward and direct, like LeeAnn herself, and they made his heart stutter in his chest. She paused, standing in her lacy bra and panties, her eyes and mouth serious. Jonah remained perfectly still, afraid that she would bolt if he moved too quickly.

"So beautiful," he whispered, drinking in every inch of her long, lean, tight body.

Blinking a little, she glanced down at the scraps of lace that barely covered her, a blush heating her cheeks and a rueful smile hovering around her lips. "I know they're not very practical—not for yoga or the ranch."

Yet she had worn them, and like everything about her, her lacy undergarments told a story—this one of a woman with a secret femininity, hidden under the concealing outfits of both the yogi and the cowgirl.

It was, he suspected, a side of herself that she didn't often share with others.

Every cell of him strained toward her, demanding that he sweep her up into his arms and claim her lips—bury himself in her—but his instincts warned him that he needed to take this slowly, even as he hardened at the sight of her.

He reached out and used one finger to tilt her chin up again. "Don't apologize." He took a half step toward her, his gentle touch turning into a caress up the side of her neck and onto her cheek. She leaned into his hand, closing her eyes briefly.

"Anyway," he said, his voice turning husky with desire, "I was talking about you...not what you're wearing."

Holding his gaze with her own, she reached back and unhooked her bra, letting it slide down her arms. A small whoosh of breath escaped him at the sight of her perfectly formed breasts, and her nipples tightened under his hot look. They bounced slightly as she pushed her panties down to join the rest of the pile of clothing, and again when she pulled her ponytail down and shook her hair out.

"Your turn," she said, glancing at the jeans he still wore.

One corner of his mouth crooking up into a grin, he took the other half step toward her, closing the space between them so that barely an inch of air separated their bodies. Heat poured off her skin, surrounding him in the smell of her—sweet sunshine and spring breeze, and a hint of vanilla, even through the faint dusty overlay of the time she'd spent in the attic.

When he reached down to unbutton his jeans, his knuckles grazed her abdomen, which quivered in response. Holding her gaze, he slid the jeans and boxers down, then reached out and pulled the shower curtain aside as he stepped out of the pants.

"Ladies first," he said.

Moving slowly, Lee Ann stepped over the high side of the claw-foot tub and knelt to turn on the water. As she stood up, her gaze flicked down at him, and her eyes widened a bit as she saw the effect her every move had on him.

When she switched over to the shower, warm water sluiced across her shoulders and down across those perfect breasts. She reached for a bottle of shampoo, but he stopped her. "Let me," he said in a voice rough with desire.

Pouring a dollop into his palm, he smoothed it across her dampened hair, then rubbed his fingers into her scalp. She closed her eyes as he pooled her hair into his hand, allowing the water to wash away the suds.

She reached up to help him, but he pushed her arm back down. "Wait," he whispered. He pulled her toward him a bit so she stepped out of the direct line of the spray. A fine mist drifted across them both.

A bottle of body wash stood on the tiny shelf next to the shampoo, so he picked it up and poured a small amount directly onto her collarbone. She gasped aloud when his fingers followed, brushing the slick soap up her neck and then down into her cleavage, never touching the sensitive buds straining toward him. Then he knelt, rubbing across her belly and down her legs, ending with her toes.

"Turn around," he said quietly.

Her breath quickened as she followed his command.

With another handful of body wash, he moved up her legs, brushing gently across her ass, then smoothing his hands across her back. Stepping up close behind her, he let his chest brush up against her back and ran his cheek against her neck while he reached around to cup her breasts. She arched up against him, standing on her toes until his cock rested in the hollow between her ass cheeks. When she moved back down to her heels, the soap he had applied all over her hot, tight body slicked against him. With a moan, he lightly pinched the tight buds and was rewarded with a gasp and another slide up and down, from the small of her back to the top of her ass, then returning to her back.

The next time she drew up onto her toes, he slid one hand down the front of her body and pulled her back against him, both palms splayed out to hold her in place—one directly in between her breasts, the other slightly above her pelvis. She pushed herself against him even harder, sliding side to side sinuously in his hands. He reached down until the tip of his middle finger barely pressed against her clit, and she whimpered. The sound went straight through him—he didn't think it was possible to get any harder than he already was, but he'd been wrong.

Sliding one leg between hers, Jonah moved them both forward into the water spray. With her weight resting on his thigh, he was able to slip his hand lower, circling her clit with his thumb while he slipped his finger down lower. For an instant, he couldn't tell if the warm wetness against his fingers was her or the water, but then his finger slipped inside her, and there was no doubt—it was all beautifully, gloriously LeeAnn. She cried out softly and arched against him, trying to touch the ground with her toes to slide up and down again, but he held her in place. "Be still," he whispered against her ear.

LeeAnn whimpered, but stopped moving. Gently, he used the leg she rested on to rock her back and forth. Every forward motion brought her clit up against his thumb as it circled, while his finger slipped deep inside her. Every backward motion brought her back against his hard cock, and he flicked his other fingers across her breasts, the taut buds growing ever tighter under his touch.

Warm water slid down their bodies, adding to the slip of skin against skin. LeeAnn's breath grew harsh, and she threw her head back. Jonah licked the exposed side of her neck, then sank his teeth lightly into her shoulder, increasing the tempo of his finger sliding in and out of her hot wetness. She matched his rhythm, slapping herself down against him until suddenly she convulsed around him, crying out as he pulled her closer.

• • •

LeeAnn came back to herself slowly, as Jonah slipped his finger out of her and slid her down his leg to stand on her own—admittedly shaky—legs.

"My turn," she said, flashing a wicked grin in his direction. For a moment, though, she stood still, distracted by the glorious body in front of her.

He was absolutely magnificent.

His blue-black hair glinted under the water. He took up most of the space in her tiny bathroom, all but filling up the old claw-foot bathtub. And what space he didn't take up physically was somehow still filled by his presence.

She couldn't stop herself from running her palm across the dusting of dark hair on his broad chest, then following it with her finger down his stomach. He shivered at her touch, and she smiled again.

"Yeah, definitely my turn," she repeated, soaping up her hands and sliding them across his shoulders, then down his arms. His biceps twitched as she moved back over them. She followed his lead, soaping up every part of him other than that one part that she knew—could see—was aching to be touched.

"Be still," she whispered when he tried to take her in his arms. The strain of it showed in his clenched jaw, but he nodded.

When she finally knelt in front of him to take him into her hands, he groaned. And when she began circling around the head of his cock with her thumb, his knees shook, and finally he took her shoulders and pulled her up, crushing her to his chest as his mouth claimed hers. His tongue swiped across her lips, and she opened herself to him.

"Wait," she said, pulling back after a long moment. She leaned out of the shower and balanced one arm on the sink, reaching into the medicine cabinet above. Foil packet in hand, she knelt again, reveling in the feel of his muscles jumping under the fingers she trailed down his chest and thigh. Without taking her gaze away from his, she unrolled the condom down over him.

With a sudden, rough motion, Jonah pulled her up against him, lifting and turning so her back was against the tile wall. She stepped up onto the edge of the tub, balancing lightly, giving him access to ever more of herself. Wrapping one leg around his waist and both arms around his neck, she waited until she felt his hand guiding his cock to her slick opening.

"Ready?" she asked.

"God, yes," he groaned.

"Hold on to me." As his grip on her tightened, she slowly lifted her other leg so that it rested over his shoulder, even as she slid down on him, taking in every last amazing inch. When she was settled against the base of his cock, she stared into his eyes.

"Don't move," she said. Taking his utter stillness as her answer, she began to pull herself up and down, using her own strength against his solid mass to move, dancing against him, over him, around him, taking him in as deep as she could, then raising up so that only the barest tip remained inside her. With every stroke, he grew harder and thicker, his breath harsh against her. The warm water sluiced across them.

After a moment, he reached out to steady himself against the wall, his arms shaking with the effort of holding still.

"Now," she said, dropping herself onto him and leaning her head back against the tile, "move."

The power in his first thrust took her breath away as he slammed into her. She met him stroke for stroke, the pressure building again inside her. He dropped one hand to cradle her ass—protecting her from the hard tiles even as he pounded into her, and this realization sent her tumbling over the edge, pleasure throbbing throughout her entire body as she shuddered, calling out his name.

At the sound of her hoarse scream, Jonah's movements became almost frenzied until he, too, pulsed and came, muffling his own cry in the crook of her neck.

They grasped one another tightly for another moment, and then Jonah gently withdrew. LeeAnn took the opportunity to unwind her legs from around him, sliding gracefully down until she stood flat-footed on the bottom of the tub.

"Holy shit, you're flexible," Jonah muttered, and she laughed out loud.

She ducked under the water for a moment, then stepped

out of the tub entirely, wrapping a towel around her and gathering up her dusty clothes from the bathroom floor. As she opened the bathroom door, she shot him a grin over her shoulder. "Yeah? Wait until you see what I can do upside down."

Laughing again, this time at the audible hitch in his breath at her comment, she stepped out into the hallway. "I'll see you in the bedroom whenever you're ready, Superman."

Chapter Twenty-One

"Wow." The word whooshed out as LeeAnn collapsed on top of him, a sentiment Jonah fully agreed with. When she nuzzled his neck, he wrapped his arms around her and rolled over so they were face-to-face.

She smiled slightly, drawing in breath to speak. Watching her eyelids flutter, Jonah waited for some commentary on how good they were together.

Because that was incredible.

Instead, LeeAnn said, "I'm starving. Are you hungry?"

A crack of laughter shot out of him, and he pulled her closer. "You are amazing," he said. "I never know what to expect."

"Whatever, Hamilton." A grin crooked up one corner of her mouth. "Are you hungry? 'Cause I want ice cream."

"You have any here?" He folded his arms behind his head.

"I'll go get it." She slid out of bed, and he marveled again at how beautiful she was—every inch of her—long and muscled and toned, hiding a softness inside that had surprised him and drawn him to her.

Jonah smiled at the sway in LeeAnn's hips as she left the room, fairly certain that the extra motion was meant to grab his attention.

It worked.

Maybe he could convince her that another shower session was in order.

Rolling over, Jonah stared out the window closest to him. The view stretched all the way back to the corner of the ranch where he had fixed the fence.

Dishes clanked in the kitchen, and he smiled again. In fact, he was pretty certain he might never quit smiling. Practically every waking moment found him thinking of her—and now he didn't have to fight it any longer.

I can tell Natural Shale that we didn't find anything, she can turn down their offer again, and I can move to my next assignment.

As his gaze drifted around the room, it caught on a small pile of papers on the bedside table.

They looked like something from the attic.

Were they? And if so, why hadn't she shown them to him?

Sitting up, he reached out and snagged the stack from their spot beside the lamp. He fanned out the documents in his hand, and as he did, a piece of yellowed paper fluttered down to the quilt covering his legs.

As it floated down to the floor, he saw two words, seemingly highlighted by the sunbeam shining through the window.

…drilling rights…

Time froze, and so did Jonah. This was the information

he'd been looking for.

Was there a reason LeeAnn had put this in her bedroom—the one place he had seemed least likely to end up? Would she hide the truth from him?

Possibly. If it meant saving her ranch from the evil oil and gas company she hated so much.

Without taking his eyes off those two potentially damning words, he scooped up the paper and angled the letter to better read the faded ink and spiked handwriting. It was dated 1989, addressed to LeeAnn's mother. Skimming down the page, he reached the words he had seen as the paper drifted by on its way to the floor.

As for the inheritance: I know you are concerned about the latest request from Belton Oil to drill on the land. Rest assured, I won't sell them the drilling rights. I didn't know they were mine until I got your letter, but Grandfather's legacy will remain untouched. In fact, I will transfer the rights to my daughters next week—I want them to have as much of a stake in the land as we do.

He flipped it over, searching for a signature, but the letter ended mid-paragraph. Hurriedly, he shuffled through the remaining papers.

Nothing.

Still, "Grandfather's legacy"? That suggested LeeAnn's uncle George, and backed up the letter the Natural Shale lawyers already held.

Mentally, he ran through the genealogical information he had unearthed at the courthouse. If the mineral rights had gone to George, then the daughters in the letter would be LeeAnn's cousins Sami and Beverly.

In any case, this was more evidence that the rights didn't belong to LeeAnn.

And given what he had heard of Sami's situation, she would probably welcome the income a drilling lease could offer. He would present it that way—as a chance to get out of her current job—and she would almost certainly jump at the opportunity.

He stared at the letter.

Could LeeAnn have had it in here—*in her bedroom, for Chrissakes*—the whole time? He pressed his fingertips against his forehead.

Damn hippies. Flakes, every last one of them.

Had he really been seduced into thinking she was any better? That their differences didn't matter?

What an idiot.

He gritted his teeth. It didn't matter what she wanted. If she couldn't even be depended on to check the pile of papers on her own nightstand, then she was too unreliable for him.

He was here to do a job, he reminded himself. Not sex up the landowner.

Jesus. What had he been thinking? That move could have cost him his promotion—could have cost him his job. Hell, it could have cost him his whole career.

And now, that job required him to take an offer to Sami.

No matter how much it upsets LeeAnn.

He dismissed the thought. It didn't matter what LeeAnn wanted. Folding the letter carefully, he grabbed his pants from the floor and pulled them on. He needed to get back to town as quickly as possible.

LeeAnn would have to drive him back to his truck, he realized as he heard her moving back toward the bedroom, humming.

Should he tell her what he had found?

Or should he simply make the offer to Sami and her sister?

He rubbed his eyes and shook his head. Apparently, at some point he had begun to believe LeeAnn's adamant assertions that the rights couldn't have been severed from the title.

And they might not have been—not legally, anyway.

Not yet.

But, assuming he could prove who wrote it, this letter would definitely serve as the legal basis for action. Natural Shale Oil and Gas could begin moving it through the court system, proving the intent to pass the drilling rights down to Sami and Beverly. And eventually, they would win.

He tried not to consider what it would mean for LeeAnn.

The sex was a distraction, he reminded himself. He had a goal, and this paper got him one step closer to that goal. As soon as he settled the rights, the promotion was his.

So. Should he tell her he had found the letter?

No. If she was too flaky to discover it herself, then she could find out about it after he'd done his job. He didn't owe her anything.

Anger pulsed through his head, hot and heavy. Jonah tried to ignore the fact that it was directed as much at himself as at LeeAnn.

By the time she reached the doorway, he was fully dressed, the fragile paper tucked carefully away in his shirt pocket.

"Something's come up," he said. "Could you take me back to town?"

Chapter Twenty-Two

"Now lean toward the door. Stretch your arms as far up and out as you can. Breathe in, then out." The words came out almost on autopilot as LeeAnn led the class in the cool-down stretches.

She couldn't quit thinking about Jonah's strange attitude all the way back into town. He had hardly spoken a word, and she could see a muscle jumping in his jaw when she asked if he wanted to join her for dinner after her class. His curt "No, thanks" didn't really come as a surprise given his body language, but she still couldn't figure out what was going on with him.

"Lie down on your mats," she said, sitting down and folding her own legs into lotus position. Although she couldn't quite bring herself to focus on the meditation and breathing exercises, she felt certain none of the students recognized her inner turmoil.

That was one thing she'd learned in her yoga training:

how to look unruffled.

No matter how she really felt.

As the students rolled up their mats and began filing out of class, she unplugged her phone from the wall where she had been charging it and glanced down to see a text from Sami.

"Call me ASAP," it said.

Her stomach sank. It was an odd message—Sami wasn't the sort to be vague, and she wouldn't request a call if it weren't serious. Had something happened to Beverly?

She hit Sami's number and held the phone to her ear, waving as the last student left the room.

Sami didn't even say hello. "I'm so glad you called."

"Hey, cuz," LeeAnn said. "What's up? You okay?"

"I am, but I think you need to come over here." Her voice sounded oddly stretched.

LeeAnn's anxiety ratcheted up. "Of course. Any hints?"

The words came out in a rush as Sami spoke. "Jonah Hamilton just left my house. He says the mineral rights belong to me and Bev, and Natural Shale Oil and Gas has made an offer."

All the blood drained from LeeAnn's face, pooling, it seemed, in her chest, constricting her lungs. After a long moment, she dragged in a breath. "Do you know why he thinks that?"

"He said he'd found another letter." Sami's voice echoed apologetically across the line. "I think you should come over."

Pacing back and forth in front of the overstuffed couch where Sami sat in her tiny apartment, LeeAnn stared at the photocopy of the letter on the coffee table. Her gaze moved back and forth between it and the offer letter sitting next to it.

"That's an awful lot of money," she said, her voice flat.

"I know," Sami almost whispered.

"That rat bastard." LeeAnn hit the end of the room and spun around, hard and fast, stomping toward the other wall, fewer than ten paces away.

Sami's anxious voice followed her. "I can't turn it down, Lee. I'm about two weeks from busted—Bev and I are still paying off Daddy's funeral, my car payment is late, not to mention my rent, and I don't know how much longer I can work in the same office with Alexander now that I know he's married."

A harsh laugh escaped LeeAnn as she finally came to a stop in front of the coffee table. "We sure do know how to pick 'em, don't we?"

"I'm so sorry." Her cousin's hands twisted together.

Panic spiked through the misery LeeAnn had felt since she'd arrived. "You can't take it, Sami. We can't let him— them, the oil company—win. Gran would hate it." As soon as she spoke, she wanted to pull the words back in—it wasn't fair to Sami.

This isn't fair to me.

And through the misery and panic ran a ribbon of bright, hot anger. Was this why Jonah had seduced her that afternoon? Had he found the letter, then decided to…what?

Distract me.

At the very least, keep her from interfering—keep her

busy until it was time for her class, then make his offer to Sami when she couldn't intervene. It all made sense. Even the weird, silent ride back into town together.

And she'd thought Darrell had been bad.

Well, okay, Darrell was awful. But Jonah was every bit as terrible.

Talk about knowing how to pick 'em.

Tears welled up in her eyes. Sami, mistaking the tears for an expression of sorrow over the land, was quick to respond. "I won't, LeeAnn. I won't take the offer. I know how much the ranch means to you, and I would never do anything to hurt you."

The whole situation is unfair to everyone except Jonah.

LeeAnn could change that—at least a little. Brushing the water from her eyes and pushing all other thoughts from her mind, she shook her head. "No," she said to her cousin. "I was wrong. You can't say no to the money." She turned to look Sami in the eye, working to make her voice clear and firm. "I don't want you to turn it down. I want you and Bev to take the offer and the money. Pay off all those bills and take some time to find another job."

"But what about the ranch? Gran would be so disappointed." A desperate note wove its way into the objection.

"Gran would want you to be taken care of, too." LeeAnn was certain of that, even if everything else in her world was falling down around her.

Still threading her fingers together as she, too, stared at the offer, Sami said, for the second time since LeeAnn's arrival, "Jonah said it would take a few weeks for everything to be finalized. Maybe I'll figure something else out between now and then."

Jonah said. Pain stabbed through LeeAnn's chest, and she abruptly stood up. "I need to get back home."

"No. Wait." Sami sat straight up. "I have an idea. Let me make a phone call."

• • •

The next morning, LeeAnn sat with her hands tightly clenched together in her lap, gritting her teeth. Sami had reached out to her boss, an attorney, and he had offered to go over the paperwork with them both to make sure they understood their options.

LeeAnn had spent the whole night tossing and turning, trying to ignore the scent of Jonah still on her sheets, trying to avoid thinking about what he had done. Finally, she had gotten up and changed the linens, tossing the Jonah-fragranced ones into the washing machine, turning the water on hot and choosing the high-speed cycle, ignoring the eco setting entirely. She had finally gotten a few hours' sleep after that.

Now, although she knew she should be preparing to listen carefully, she couldn't help but consider Alexander J. Wills, Esq., as he sat behind his extraordinarily shiny chrome-and-glass desk reading through everything they had brought.

So this is the man who seduced my cousin?

He wasn't LeeAnn's type, for sure—far too skinny white boy, as Sami's friend Martina would say, all lines and angles, his brown eyes serious behind his glasses as he flipped through the stack of papers in front of him with long, pale, ascetic-looking fingers.

Contrasting Wills's to Jonah's muscular virility came to

her all too easily, and LeeAnn cursed silently. She needed to get Jonah out of her mind. He hadn't meant anything he said. The fact that she was here, trying to determine if she had any legal recourse to keep Natural Shale off her land, was proof enough of that.

Finally, the attorney leaned back in his chair and peered at the two women over the rim of his glasses. "It looks here like Natural Shale is banking on you, Ms. Walker, not putting up a real fight. There is currently no official record of the mineral rights having been explicitly severed from the property title. However, the company has in its possession two documents that suggest that by the late 1990s, at least, the mineral rights belonged to George McKinley, Samantha's father."

Sami winced a little at Wills's use of her full name.

He has to know she hates that. What kind of man would call her by a name he knows she hates?

Then again, what kind of married man would date his new secretary without telling her he was married?

Untangling her hands, LeeAnn leaned forward. "What are our options?"

Wills took off his glasses, folded them carefully, and rapped them gently against the desk. "As I see it, you have four options. One, you can waive the rights, leaving them to Samantha and her...sister, was it?" He flipped his index finger out and gave it a slight wave.

"Beverly, yes." Sami nodded, glancing at LeeAnn out of the corner of her eye, gauging her reaction to the possibility. LeeAnn worked to keep her face expressionless.

Breathe in...one, two, three...out, one, two, three, four...

Adding a second long finger, Wills said, "Two, Samantha

and Beverly can waive the rights, leaving them with you, but thereby giving up a sizable rental income that could, under these contracts, increase significantly if any wells are successful. And three, you could both claim the rights, and the whole thing can go to court."

Wills dropped his hand back to his glasses and picked them up. The tapping noise he made lodged itself behind LeeAnn's right eye, where she could feel a headache forming, throbbing in time to Wills's taps.

She rubbed her fingertips against her temples. "Do you mean go to court against each other?"

Wills shrugged. "Possibly. Though Samantha will undoubtedly benefit from Natural Shale's backing."

"Are you saying I would lose, just because they have a couple of letters?" The pounding in her head picked up tempo.

He shrugged and unfolded the glasses. When they were again perched on his nose, he pulled the two letters out of the papers and placed them side by side. "Not necessarily. If letters were enough to guarantee a victory, they would have gone straight for a court date, rather than trying a work-around like getting their landman into your files."

Right. So if she hadn't taken Jonah at his word, hadn't believed him enough to let him onto her land, into her home…

…into my bed…

If she hadn't trusted him, she wouldn't be in this position.

"And now?" she asked, trying to keep her voice steady.

Wills shrugged. "Now they have two points of data. They know it's worth their time and effort. They'll subpoena all your records and put their best experts on it to comb through everything."

Sami, who had been staring at the floor, absently rubbing her thumb across the pearls of one of her necklaces, sat up straighter. "You said there we had a fourth option?"

"Yes." Wills opened both hands wide, palms up, gesturing toward the women. "The two of you, along with Beverly, could come to a private agreement to split proceeds, and then all act as signatories to any agreement with Natural Shale."

LeeAnn and Sami stared at each other for a moment. LeeAnn looked away first. When she spoke again, her voice was quiet. "And the only way to get out of this without a lot of money—and trouble—is to sign over the rights and let Natural Shale drill?"

This time, his shrug included a throwaway motion of one hand. "You might be able to find an environmentalists' group to back you. And you could conceivably fight every step of the way, from drilling rights to right-of-way agreements for the trucks. But in my opinion? Yes. You're looking at a long, drawn-out fight that you are at least as likely to lose as you are to win, and that will cost you more than you might be willing to spend."

More than I can spend. More than I have.

Bending over to gather her purse, LeeAnn bit the inside of her lip to keep from crying. "Thank you, Mr. Wills," she said, holding out one hand over the desk as he rose to see her out. "Sami, I'll call you in a few days. I have a lot of thinking to do."

"Of course." Wills ushered her to the office door, but paused with his hand on the knob. "One question, if I may. If you are so opposed to drilling on your land, why did you allow one of Natural Shale's agents free access to your records?"

A harsh huff of laughter escaped her. "That's a good question, Mr. Wills."

She glanced over her shoulder, but caught only a glimpse of the misery on Sami's face before the closing door cut off her view.

Chapter Twenty-Three

Staring out over the ranch, LeeAnn raised her arms above her head and drew in a deep breath, counting silently as she breathed in and out, trying to decide what she should do. She had been here for hours. Finally, she had given up and called her cousin to ask her to come over.

By the time Sami gets here, she promised herself, *I'll have made a decision.*

But instead of calmly weighing her options yet again, she kept coming back to Jonah, even though every time she thought of him, her stomach roiled.

How could I have been so stupid?

She had talked to him about everything that mattered to her—her parents, yoga, the ranch. Everything.

She had taken him into her bed.

And shower, a wry internal voice reminded her. She pushed the memory away.

She had trusted him.

Quit thinking about Jonah. Figure out what to do about the drilling rights. Handing them over meant hurting the land. Fighting them meant hurting Sami.

She couldn't see a way to live by her principles. No matter what she did, she feared she would be hurt the worst.

Om…

She was still considering her options when the crunch of tires on caliche alerted her to her cousin's arrival.

But when Sami rounded the corner of the house, her step more tentative than LeeAnn had ever seen it, she knew what the decision had to be. It was the only possible choice — and had been, ever since Sami had shown her the offer.

Even if it broke her heart.

"I've decided to sign over the rights," she said, as soon as Sami was close enough to hear.

"You have?" The sudden brightening of Sami's eyes convinced LeeAnn she had done the right thing.

"Yes." She held out her arms to enfold Sami in a hug. "I *want* you to have the money."

Only once Sami was gone again did she allow herself to collapse onto her mat. Rubbing her eyes, she pulled in a deep, ragged breath.

Despite her resolution to move on, she found herself thinking about Jonah once more. She still couldn't believe he had found a letter and hadn't told her.

I can't believe I trusted him.

What was wrong with her? Why did she continue to get attached to men who lied and cheated and used her to get what they wanted, without any consideration for her?

First Darrell, now Jonah.

Okay. That wasn't entirely fair. Jonah hadn't ever lied —

not really. She had known from the beginning that he was trying to find a way to allow his company to drill on her property. But she had truly believed that he would tell her if he found anything.

She had allowed herself to relax around him.

She hadn't merely let him into her home. She had allowed him into her bed. And…

Oh, no. Am I really in love with Jonah?

"Dammit," she whispered, tears leaking out of the corners of her eyes. She pulled her knees up to her chest and banged her forehead gently against them, cursing with each bump.

She had known from almost the beginning that she and Jonah Hamilton were working at cross-purposes. He might not have seemed like the enemy, but he was.

It had been foolish of her to forget that.

If only she hadn't thrown herself into his arms that first day in the diner. Would she have been able to keep her distance if she had known who he was, why he was there?

Or would he have charmed her, anyway?

She was so unbelievably stupid. It had all been an act, designed to keep her from seeing what he was up to as he worked out how, precisely, to screw her out of the mineral rights.

She snorted. *Literally screw me out of them.*

She might not have been able to stop him from stealing her heart while he slipped drilling rights out from under her, but she didn't have to allow him to continue to hurt her.

Time to cowboy up, LeeAnn.

With a rueful grin, she straightened her spine, drew in a deep breath, rolled up her mat, and headed inside. At least now that she knew for sure that the rights belonged to Sami and Bev, she could quit worrying about it. And she wouldn't ever have to see Jonah Hamilton again.

No more crying.

Rebound guys don't deserve tears.

At least, that's what she told herself—for all the good it did.

No, she decided as she pulled open the door. *I need to see him one last time. This won't be like Darrell. I won't let this man lie and cheat and walk out on me without saying something.*

I'm going to tell him exactly what I think of him.

And then she would never again forget that he was not to be trusted.

No one was.

The only person she could really rely upon was herself.

But somehow, the thought rang hollow.

· · ·

Jonah stared at the text from LeeAnn on his phone: "*I need to see you.*"

The last thing he wanted was to see her again. At least, not under these circumstances.

Of course, he was going to have to deal with her one more time to get her signature on the right-of-way contract for the survey and drilling teams. And he owed her a paycheck.

This moment should have felt like victory. He was used to winning, used to his gambles paying off. It was part of why he was so good at his job.

It was why Nathan had called him that morning to let

him know that Natural Shale was definitely planning to offer him the senior landman position. The paperwork should make its way through the system in about a month.

But the elation of making the deal, closing the case, finishing the contract, reaching the goal—it was all missing, leaving behind only an empty feeling in the pit of his stomach.

God save me from any more victories like this one. I don't think I could survive it.

If he were honest with himself, he wasn't sure he was going to survive this one.

Shaking off the thought, he pulled his leather-covered checkbook out of the back pocket of his Levi's and began calculating the hours LeeAnn had spent searching through the attic. He ripped a deposit statement out of the back of the checkbook and added up the numbers, then stared at the total.

Had they really spent that much time together?

He thought back.

Six outbuildings—though we only got through three before I found the letter. Two old barns. One empty stable. One huge attic.

One shower.

One bed.

Dropping his head into his hands, he blew out a defeated breath. He had managed to avoid thinking about the shower—or the bed, for that matter—until now.

His heart sat like lead in his chest.

One more time. It wasn't fair to either of them to walk away without a word. He owed it to himself, if not to LeeAnn, to tell her that he wouldn't be back.

After a few more calculations, he wrote out the check, then carefully tore it along the perforated edge. He slipped it into a hotel envelope, scrawled her name across the front, and stared at the words for a long time before he finally grabbed his keys and left the room.

This is the last time I have to see her—and then I'll be free of her forever.

Free to go back to his life, with the promotion he'd been aiming for. More stable than ever before. In control of his life.

Without any flaky yogis to distract him from his goals.

So why did the thought of never seeing her again make his shoulders tighten in misery?

• • •

As she turned into the parking lot linking the Wagon Wheel to the rest of the block, LeeAnn scanned for Jonah's pickup.

The bright morning sunlight glinting off the windshields seemed far too cheerful for her mood today. The Stockyards District was beginning to stir, but later in the day, it would be crowded as the tourists made their way to the daily longhorn cattle drive over on Exchange Street.

Normally, this kind of spring morning would brighten everything around it.

It should be raining.

Of course he opted to meet outside, she fumed. *It makes for an easier getaway.*

Spotting an old green truck, LeeAnn veered toward it—until she spied a pair of Truck Nutz dangling from the back. Apparently whoever owned the Ford was a local. LeeAnn wondered if he had noticed the reattachment job Jonah had done on the plastic testicles.

Cursing to herself, she pulled into a spot and parked. In the last few days, she had discovered that she couldn't go anywhere without memories of Jonah popping up. It was like he had touched every part of her life.

Contaminated it.

But she didn't sound convinced, even in the confines of her own mind. No matter how angry she was, part of her still longed for him to return. Not that she would ever admit that, even to herself.

A sharp rap at her window jerked her out of her scowling reverie.

Jonah took a step back from her car and stared off at something in the distance.

Her stomach clenched, sending flutters up through her entire torso. Suddenly, she couldn't remember why she was here.

Why did I think I had to say this in person?

All she wanted to do was run away.

But I'm not the coward he is. I won't leave without telling him exactly what I think of what he's done.

Right. Putting on my big-girl panties. Again.

Om...

She could do this. All she had to do was say her piece, then get back in the car and go home, where every part of the ranch, even her house, reminded her of Jonah.

Opening the door, she stepped out onto the pavement, grounding herself through the earth, feeling the power of the entire world move up and through her.

Breathe. In, one, two, three. Out, one, two, three, four—

"You said you needed to talk to me?" Jonah's tone was brusque. LeeAnn hadn't realized how accustomed she had grown to his easy smile, his relaxed strength. Now, though, he looked furious, every line of his body tight and angry. She couldn't see his eyes, covered as they were by dark sunglasses.

He looks almost frightening.

But some part of her still knew that no matter how infuriated he might be, he would never hurt her.

Another part of her wanted to reach out and touch him, to soothe that anger away.

Instead, she folded her hands in front of her and breathed in and out before finally speaking. "I wanted you to know that the mineral rights are going to Sami and Bev. I won't be fighting it. In fact, I'm meeting with Sami's boss tomorrow—he's a lawyer—to sign some sort of paperwork saying I agree that they own the rights." She worked to keep the hitch in her throat out of her voice, to sound calm and smooth rather than ragged and exhausted.

"I'm glad to hear it." His own voice was detached and distant.

"So you didn't have to steal the letter from me." Her comment caused his head to jerk around so that he was staring directly at her.

"I didn't—" he began, but LeeAnn kept talking, right over him.

"So you can just take your sneaky romancing-the-stone bullshit and your charming dimples and your manipulative job offers and shove…"

Feeling her blood pressure beginning to rise, she closed her eyes and breathed in deeply. Somehow, talking to Jonah wasn't turning out any better than *not* talking to Darrell had.

"You know what? Never mind," she said. As she prepared to reach behind her to open the car door, she realized that she had unconsciously pulled one foot up against the other in a balancing pose.

Balance. Sometimes my body knows what I need better than my mind.

And she would certainly be better able to find more equilibrium in her life without Jonah around to send her emotions heaving, first in one direction and then another.

"Good-bye," she said as she dropped her foot to the ground and took a step backward.

"Wait," Jonah said. "We're not finished here."

• • •

Dammit all to hell. She's doing anxiety yoga again.

Jonah found himself wanting to lash out at the person making her feel awful. But of course, that person was him.

It's not my fault that her flaky yoga shit kept me from finding out who the mineral rights belonged to any sooner.

He shook his head. None of that mattered now. Fishing the envelope out of his back pocket, he thrust it toward LeeAnn.

"This is yours." She took it but watched him carefully, as if he might strike out at any moment, never even looking down to see what he had handed her.

They stared at one another in silence, and Jonah could almost imagine that he saw pain in the depths of her gray eyes.

"The company will also pay for right-of-way access," he

finally bit out, unable to keep from trying to help her, even now, when all obligations had ended.

"Thanks," she said. "I'll keep that in mind. Is that it?"

His voice dropped. "Yeah. I guess so."

Without another word, she opened her car door and got in. Jonah didn't even think about it—he simply reached out to stop her from closing it. She stared straight ahead, hands grasping the steering wheel in front of her.

Leaning into the driver's side, he said, "Actually, there is one more thing, LeeAnn. I think you should try to remember that people are the most important part of your world. You really are doing the right thing. People are more important than land. More important than principles. More important than anything."

At that, she finally turned to look at him, the lines of her face hard and unyielding. "More important than money, Jonah? More important than control? Than *getting ahead*?" The final words were injected with a sneer.

When she grabbed the door handle and pulled it from his grasp, Jonah let it go to slam closed and watched as the silver Prius pulled out of the parking lot and drove out of sight.

It's better this way. I don't need to get mixed up with someone like that. She's not right for me.

If only he truly believed it.

Chapter Twenty-Four

Twelve days. That's how long it had been since he had watched LeeAnn drive away.

He had considered calling a couple of times, but then he reminded himself that his work with her was finished.

He had reached his goal.

The promotion was his.

His life could start moving forward again.

That should have made him happy—he had done exactly the job that the company had hired him to do, and everyone was getting what they wanted.

Everyone except LeeAnn.

He shook off the thought. LeeAnn had wanted to find something in the attics to help out her cousins. The drilling lease was going to do exactly that.

The fact that she didn't know she had left the letter about the mineral rights on her nightstand proved, without a doubt, that she was a flaky neo-hippie without enough sense to pay attention to things in the real world.

And handing over the mineral rights to her cousins showed that she really did care about her family more than her stupid principles.

Right?

Or does she just know when she has a losing hand?

For some reason, the thought of her simply giving up made his chest ache. As angry as he had been when he found the letter, he almost wanted her to keep fighting.

In any case, Jonah had closed out the paperwork, and a new project took him out to Amarillo for a few days while Nathan worked on pushing his promotion through the system. Another few weeks, and he would be senior landman.

He was glad to get out of town.

Or at least, that's what he told himself.

The new job was a straightforward records search. A trip to the county clerk's office had yielded the information he needed, and the landowner—a cattle rancher whose herd had been wiped out by a drought a few years ago—had been happy to sign the oil lease.

Amarillo had been a breeze.

No beautiful, amazingly flexible blonde with a nervous-yoga habit had tried to distract him from doing his job in Amarillo.

Because surely that's why LeeAnn had sex with him— to keep him off balance, to keep him from finding the information he needed.

And it had worked, too.

I'm still unbalanced, dammit.

He couldn't quit thinking about her. That was part of why he was right back in Fort Worth. Ostensibly, it was to have LeeAnn sign the right-of-way waiver that would allow the survey trucks onto her ranch. Sami and Bev were having their attorney look over their drilling rights lease before they signed it—something he always suggested. If all went well, the surveyors would finish their work about the time the final papers were filed, and then the real business of drilling could begin.

For the first time since he had become a landman, the prospect didn't thrill him.

Instead, all he could think of was the frown on LeeAnn's face when she told him good-bye the last day.

So here he was, walking from his hotel to the TexZen Yoga Studio, when he could have just as easily mailed the right-of-way papers. As he turned the corner, he caught a glimpse of a blond ponytail swinging as its owner pulled open the door to the Wagon Wheel and walked in.

"LeeAnn?" he called, quickening his step. The woman didn't hear him.

That damn diner. Every time he thought of it, he remembered kissing LeeAnn. He slowed as he came even with the windows, trying to peer in. A single ray of fading sunlight glanced off the window, though, reflecting only his own image back at him.

He stepped inside, blinking to adjust to the lower light.

There, in the same booth where he had hauled her into his lap to kiss her, LeeAnn sat, leaning forward, apparently speaking to someone. Jonah's view of her dinner partner was momentarily blocked by the hostess.

"For one?" she asked.

He peered around her, going totally still when he saw who it was LeeAnn was talking to so intently.

Darrell Vincent.

The bastard who had left her for another woman.

Seriously?

She tilted her head and half smiled at something the other man said. Jonah's hands curled into fists at his side, and he fought down the urge to stride over and knock the asshole unconscious.

He took a deep breath, unclenching his fists and forcing himself to focus on the waitress.

"No, thanks," he said and left the restaurant, heading back toward his hotel.

LeeAnn was no good for him, anyway. She was unreliable. Undependable. And she had tried to distract him from his job with sex.

The best sex of your life, a tiny voice inside him whispered. He ignored it, instead focusing on what mattered: that her love life was none of his business.

But a deep ache where his heart should be suggested otherwise.

• • •

Sunlight flashed from the diner door as it closed. LeeAnn glanced toward it, then did a swift double take.

Was that Jonah, leaving?

Darrell reached out across the table and tried to touch her fingers. She drew her hand back down, into her lap, and leaned back against the red leather cushion of the booth. Apparently laughing in his face and telling him to go away when he sat down to apologize hadn't been enough to make him leave.

His dark brown eyes widened a bit, and he gazed at her imploringly. "I really mean it."

This was the same tactic he had used throughout their entire relationship: do something stupid, then look miserable enough to convince her to take pity on him.

For once, she wasn't falling for it. In fact, she was a little surprised to discover that she didn't care at all.

"Great," she said, her tone abstracted as she tried to peer out the window. "You had a lot to be sorry for."

"I made a terrible mistake. But I know that now, and I want you back," Darrell said, breaking through her distraction. "I miss you." He slid both arms across the table, stretching out as if to take her into his arms.

Shying back even farther, she began scooting out of the booth seat. "You are insane." As she stood up, she began digging in her purse, finally tossing a twenty-dollar bill down onto the table. "You're an ass-hat, Darrell." She laughed again, just a little.

His mouth fell open in shock. "What did you say to me?"

"I said, you're an ass-hat. There is nothing you could ever say that would make me want to take you back." She took two steps toward the door, then turned back to face him again. "Your fiancée broke it off, didn't she?"

"Yes." Darrell's nostrils flared as he stared at the floor.

LeeAnn laughed yet again, louder this time, and shrugged. "Well, it's no better than you deserve." She waved over her shoulder as she headed out of the restaurant, but she didn't look back.

Out on the sidewalk, she peered left and then right. Had that really been Jonah she had seen leaving the restaurant? Or a figment of her overactive imagination, giving her a glimpse of the man she would rather have sitting at her table and apologizing?

Either way, she saw no one on the sidewalk.

With a sigh, she hiked her purse up over her shoulder and began walking back toward the studio, where she had left her car.

Oh, well. Things could be worse.

She could have accepted Darrell's apology, for example.

She snorted in quiet laughter.

No. I could never accept Darrell—or anyone like him—again.

Though to be honest, she would have expected to get more satisfaction out of Darrell's misery. It was hard to stay too angry at someone she cared about so very little. Jonah, on the other hand? She was still furious with him for picking up and leaving town without saying another word to her.

Once he had found the letter, Jonah had no further use for her.

She understood that, and it made her breathlessly angry.

But doesn't that anger mean I still care about him?

Her heart constricted in her chest.

She couldn't even bring herself to call him names—not aloud, not in the privacy of her own mind.

She loved him too much for that.

But I can get over it, given enough time.

With a sigh, she pulled her key fob out of her purse to unlock her car and saw a manila envelope tucked under the windshield wipers. Puzzled, she drew it out. A note was scribbled on the back: *Please sign and return. —J*

It *had* been Jonah she had seen leaving the restaurant.

Tears swam in her eyes, blurring her vision. He couldn't

even be bothered to give her the papers in person.

He truly doesn't care about me.

It really was all an act. He wanted the mineral rights more than he ever wanted me.

She hadn't been willing to admit that any part of her believed he might have actually cared—but the misery she felt suggested that she'd hoped, at least subconsciously, that he might come back, might tell her it had all been a mistake.

How could she have believed anything he said? How could she have trusted him?

Stupid, stupid, stupid. You knew all along what he was here for.

It was all her own fault for forgetting, even for an instant, that Jonah was the enemy, out to take her world away from her.

And he succeeded, too.

Her heart felt like it was cracking inside her chest, and no amount of yoga would ever help her heal from it.

There's no pose for this kind of pain.

But I need to move past this.

There had to be a way. After all, she'd gotten over Darrell pretty quickly, all things considered. Then again, Darrell was the king of ass-hats. But her breakup with him had left her open to Jonah's charm.

I will never be that vulnerable again.

Blinking away the tears, she opened her car door and dropped the papers into the passenger seat.

Time, she told herself. That's all she needed.

But honestly? She wasn't sure there would ever be enough time to get over Jonah.

Chapter Twenty-Five

The buzz of his cell phone woke Jonah the next morning. Rubbing his eyes, he rolled over to grab it and tried to shake off the deeply erotic dream he'd been having about an upside-down LeeAnn.

He squinted at the phone in the half dark of the hotel room, then blinked when he saw the time. He needed to get moving if he was going to check out today and head back home.

Home. Right.

A lonely apartment in Midland.

He began to scroll through his texts. Maybe Natural Shale had a new job for him already, and he could skip going back to Midland altogether.

His boss Nathan had indeed sent him a message, but not one that would send him away—not quite yet, anyway. Apparently LeeAnn had faxed the signed paperwork over to the main office the day before. Sami and Bev still hadn't sent their signed copies, so Nathan had asked him to contact Sami.

In person would probably be better.

He flinched at the next thought that came unbidden: *Or at least more likely to allow me to turn the conversation to LeeAnn and her reunion with Darrell Vincent.*

Shaking his head, he rolled out of bed and headed toward the shower.

Before he got a signature from Sami, he would schedule the final survey team to go out to the ranch—and then he could leave Fort Worth behind him, at least for a while.

. . .

"Come on in," Sami said, ushering Jonah into her tiny apartment. He'd been glad, but a little surprised, to find her at home at three in the afternoon. He might have assumed that she had left work and come home for a late lunch break, if not for the fact that she was still in pajamas and a robe and had daytime television playing in the postage stamp–sized living room.

"Is this a bad time?" he asked.

"Not really," she said. "I...took the day off." She tightened the belt of the robe and crossed her arms.

Remembering Sami's discussion with LeeAnn over the barbecue grill, Jonah refrained from asking any more questions. Instead, he chose to broach the subject that brought him to her apartment. "My boss asked me to stop by and pick up the contract," he said, pitching his voice somewhere between a question and a statement.

"Right. I'm having one of the attorneys at work look

it over. That's not a problem, is it? She said she'd probably have it done by tomorrow." As small as she was, her worried expression made her look especially childlike.

"Not a problem at all," he replied. "Do you know if she has any questions? I can get the new survey team out to the ranch tomorrow, but I don't want to try to schedule drilling until we have the contract in hand."

"Tomorrow?" Sami asked, startled. "Does LeeAnn know?"

I wish I hadn't mentioned that part.

Usually he was much more careful about the words that came out of his mouth. But apparently everything about LeeAnn—even dealing with her tiny cousin—rattled him.

He tried to gather his thoughts. "She signed the right-of-way contract, so…" He shrugged.

Sami nodded, wincing a little—presumably at the thought of the yoga instructor's reaction to trucks barreling across her land. "Let me call Teresa and see where she is on the contract."

She left the room, and Jonah glanced around, his gaze snagging on a shelf full of family photos. He moved closer, searching for pictures of LeeAnn.

There she was, standing at another backyard party at her place, her head thrown back, mouth open in laughter. His heart squeezed in his chest.

She's so beautiful.

Next to her in the photo stood Darrell Vincent, a supercilious smile on his face.

"Isn't that a great photo of LeeAnn?" Sami entered the room, phone in hand. "She hates it, but it's one of my favorites." Pausing beside him, she brushed a speck of dust from the brass frame. Her voice hardened. "Of course, it would be even better if that jackass wasn't in it."

Jonah worked to keep his tone casual. "You mean Darrell? Aren't they seeing each other again?"

Sami's laugh filled the small space. "No way. He came begging back, but LeeAnn sent him packing."

The rushing noise that filled his ears blocked out the next few words.

LeeAnn wasn't with Darrell Vincent?

Suddenly, Jonah felt lighter, as a cloud he hadn't even known was hovering over his heart lifted.

"So anyway," Sami said, "Teresa says the contract should be ready in the next few days. I'll get Bev to sign her copy and fax it, too."

He nodded, fighting an inappropriate urge to grin.

"Thanks so much," Sami said as she ushered him to the door. "LeeAnn says you're the one who found the letter. If you hadn't, we might never have known that the rights belonged to Bev and me. Every time I try to thank her, she says it's all because of you."

"She does?" Stepping outside, he turned back to face Sami.

"Yeah. You really saved me. The letter was under some stuff on her bedside table, right? She said she dropped it there when I called about that party." An impish grin lit up her face. "But she won't tell me what you were doing in her bedroom when you found it." With a wink, she shut the door, leaving Jonah standing outside, trying to work through all the implications of Sami's words.

LeeAnn isn't dating Vincent.

And if I am wrong about that…then what else might I be wrong about?

Back in his hotel room, Jonah paced the length of the room, trying to decide what to do next.

So what if LeeAnn wasn't seeing her ex again?

What does that change?

She clearly didn't care about the important things in life. She was still too flaky to be trusted with important papers. And she was still wrong for him in almost every way—too vegetarian, too hippie chick, too…too…

He froze, stunned by the thoughts that came next.

Too concerned with her family to let her ideals interfere with their needs.

Too kind to let an abandoned horse remain homeless.

Too caring to allow an injury—even a scratch from a mesquite tree—stay unbandaged.

Too generous to say no when her cousin asked for a spirit-lifting barbecue on the ranch.

Too helpful to try to find a better job when her friend needed someone to watch the store.

Too strong to go back to someone who hurt her as badly as Vincent did. As badly as I did?

Finally, he admitted it to himself. What did the fact that she wasn't seeing her ex again change?

Everything.

Because his life looked grim without her in it—an endless round of drilling rights negotiations, punctuated by dreary hotels rooms and lonely nights.

Sure, he would get the promotion. A better title. More money.

But why did he need it? To take care of his father? His dad's tiny house had been paid off for years, and truth be told, it didn't cost Jonah all that much to support him. His own apartment? There was nothing holding him there.

The thought of continuing as he was made his heart sink.

So what about a future with LeeAnn? The idea caused him to freeze in sheer terror for an instant. Spend his life with someone that unpredictable?

But then he tried to picture it, and the images unfolded in bright colors. Horseback riding. Fixing her fences. Buttermilk pie at the Wagon Wheel Diner. Yoga classes. Her beautiful gray eyes, sparkling up at him.

He'd spent years building his career, resenting his father for being a burden. Earning money, but never really using it to *live*.

And he'd shoved away the one person who had given him a glimpse of what living life could really be like.

Could he ever possibly win back her trust?

Maybe even her love?

Almost as soon as that thought finished, a plan sprang into his mind, as if it had been waiting in his subconscious for the right moment to leap out at him.

"Oh," he whispered. "That's perfect."

He glanced at the clock, running through everything he'd have to do.

There was no way he could finish all the steps before Natural Shale shut down for the evening.

But I can definitely get started.

Moving as quickly as possible, he snagged his phone from the desk, prepared to dial. But then he saw the text that had arrived while he paced. It was from Jenny, his librarian friend in West Texas.

She had found a buyer for some of the magazines he'd been snapping pictures of for the last several weeks. As he read the rest of the message, he began laughing aloud.

"Jenny," he texted, *"your timing is perfect."*

Then he dialed. "Nathan," he said when his boss answered. "We need to talk."

Chapter Twenty-Six

The heavy grinding sound of the trucks' engines made Lee-Ann wince as she stepped out onto the front porch. They had shown up earlier than she had anticipated, interrupting her morning practice. Squinting into the sun, she watched the small convoy as it trundled across her land.

A dually pickup bounced over the caliche road and turned off the path to lead the way down to the lower pasture. The other trucks followed, smashing bluebonnets and wildflowers under their heavy tread. Closing her eyes, Lee-Ann drew in a deep breath, then coughed at the residual exhaust in the air.

At least they were following the directions she had given them on the phone—they weren't trampling her vegetable garden or her cultivated flowers.

This is important to Sami and Bev, she reminded herself. *They need the money more than I need to leave the land untouched.*

If it helped them, even the horrible trucks crawling all over her ranch would be worth it.

People really are more important than principles, she reminded herself.

But tears still gathered in the corners of her eyes.

I ought to go saddle up Blackie.

When the trucks finally stopped, several men got out, pulling out surveying equipment and setting up tripods as they peered through some sort of lenses.

Wrapping her arms around her shoulders, she headed back into the house and perched on the edge of the living room sofa. Just because she had said they could get started early didn't mean she had to watch them.

In fact, she didn't have to allow them on the land at all— not yet, anyway. Sami had told her that she and Bev hadn't actually signed the drilling lease yet.

But I signed the right-of-way contract.

Natural Shale had asked if they could get started. Apparently their survey team's work was unusually light this week.

The sooner they got started, the sooner Sami and Bev would begin getting paid. She wasn't about to delay that, even if the thought of the potential damage that drilling could do to the ranchland broke her heart.

At least, it would have broken her heart if it weren't already shattered into tiny pieces.

She'd thought she'd been miserable when she found out Darrell had been cheating on her. Now, though, she recognized that feeling as simply wounded pride, producing the kind of anger that left her cursing his name.

Her reaction to Darrell's lies had nothing on how she

felt now.

Misery didn't really cover it.

Absolutely devastated came closer.

Heartsick.

She had yet to find a yoga pose that could help with that.

When Sami had called, trying to prod her cousin into saying something by telling her that Jonah had come by, LeeAnn hadn't been able to work up enough resentment for name-calling.

She didn't have any pride left to be wounded. Even if Jonah had no interest in her, she wanted to hear it directly from him.

But even when she'd overcome her fear enough to dial his number the night before, he didn't return the call.

There were things she needed to say to him, though.

She needed to tell him she wasn't angry that he had found the letter—that she could be okay with the drilling, if only he were here with her.

She needed to ask him if she had ever been more to him than just a job.

She wanted to tell him how she really felt about him, to tell him that she loved him, despite everything.

Was she stupid to even consider trusting him again? Possibly. But the more she'd thought about his last words to her—*people are more important than principles*—the more she'd realized he was right.

Her principles had protected her for a long time, helped her heal from her parents' deaths and her uncle's lies. They hadn't kept her heart safe from Jonah, though. Maybe that was a good thing.

Maybe she couldn't ever really connect with someone

else unless she figured out how to trust someone other than herself.

With a groan, she pushed herself up again.

What she needed was to get out of her own head. As usual, she was thinking far too much.

Reaching into the top of the entryway closet, she pulled down the mat she used outside. Yoga would clear her mind— or at least help her focus on something else for a while.

After she was done, she would push past the terror clutching her stomach and sit down to write Jonah a letter. He might never answer, but at least she would know she had done everything possible to let him know how she felt. To begin to learn how to trust again.

· · ·

Jonah navigated his pickup through the narrow gate onto the driveway leading to LeeAnn's house, bouncing in the seat as the tires rumbled over the cattle guard.

He glanced down at the notification of a voicemail message on his phone one last time, still not fully trusting his eyes.

The grin he hadn't been able to shake all morning faltered a bit. Surely LeeAnn would forgive his silence once she found out what he'd been doing.

As he rounded the bend in the drive and the house came into view, he caught a glimpse of her on the slight hill beside the house, stretching her arms into the air before bending over in a fluid, graceful motion.

She is stunning.

His heart constricted at the thought that she might not

want to see him.

The sight of the survey team working out in the pasture did nothing to calm his nerves.

But they wouldn't be a problem for much longer. And no matter what, he would not leave again.

Not if he had anything to say about it.

Stopping in front of the house, he parked the truck and jumped to the ground. Watching for LeeAnn, he moved around the house.

Surely she had seen him driving up.

When he turned the corner, he found her sitting cross-legged, eyes closed, hands placed palm up on her knees. For a long, quiet moment, he simply watched her breathe.

He could do that forever.

"Can we talk?" he finally asked, quietly.

She opened her eyes. "It might take a while," she said. "I have a lot to say."

He nodded. "Okay. But can I say one thing first?"

"Okay." She breathed deeply, as if preparing for a physical blow.

Pulling his phone out of his pocket, he dropped the file folder he carried onto the ground. Then he lowered himself gently to the mat beside her, digging the heels of his boots into the grass in front of him, and flipped through the messages until he found the one he wanted. "Here," he said, unable to hide the smile in his voice.

She read the text, blinked and shook her head, then read it again.

"Wait," she said, her eyes growing huge as she looked up at him. "Is that number right?"

His smile stretched wider. "It is exactly right."

"Who would pay that much for a bunch of old magazines?" She looked back and forth between him and the phone.

"Apparently some of the older ones are incredibly rare and valuable." He took the phone away from her and flipped through some of the pictures. "I think you'll appreciate this one, in particular."

At least, he hoped she did. A smile from her might make the next part of what he planned to say easier. Waiting for her to take the phone he held out, he felt his stomach tighten into knots.

When she finally glanced down at the picture on the screen, a crack of laughter shot out of her. "A Superman *TV Guide*?" she asked incredulously.

"George Reeves, from 1953. That one all by itself is worth about a thousand dollars." He stood up and held his hand out to her. "The library my friend works for is willing to shell out about three-quarters of the total price for all of them right now, or you can auction them off and potentially get even more."

Absently, still staring at the image on the phone, she took his fingers in hers to stand. As soon as she touched him, an electric spark shot straight from his arm to his heart. Her slight jump suggested she felt it, too. She stepped away from him and looked down at his phone again.

"That's more than the oil lease," she said slowly.

He nodded. "Enough to take care of Sami and Bev and have money left over."

"I need to call them." Her gaze upon him was steady, but wary.

"You *could* use the money to buy the mineral rights back from them, if you wanted." He took a step toward her.

She paused, her gaze turning suspicious. "But?" She blinked, and her expression changed to panic. "Is it too late?" she asked.

He shook his head. "No. That's not it at all. In fact, I talked to Sami last night."

"And?"

Taking a deep breath, he closed his eyes for an instant, then came out with it. "And I bought the rights from her myself."

Her hands flew up to cover her mouth as she gasped, and she crumpled to the mat in a heap. "Oh, God. How could you?"

Jonah dropped to his knees beside her, pulled as if by a magnet, drawn to comfort her. "No, LeeAnn. Not for Natural Shale. Not to drill." He laughed a little as he gently pulled her hands away from her eyes, softening his voice to match his touch. "I realized I could never do that to you."

She blinked at him doubtfully, her eyes a stormy gray.

He could stare into those eyes forever.

But not if I don't explain myself soon.

Scooping up the folder from the ground, he handed it to her, then watched as she skimmed the papers inside. "It's all yours," he said. "The papers are signed and notarized, and Sami's boss is on his way to register the transfer with the county."

She glanced down at the paper one more time. "Won't you get in trouble with your company?"

"Not my company anymore. I quit, right before I called Sami."

"You *what*? Why? What about your father? Your promotion? What will you do?" Her questions tumbled over one another, even as she stood perfectly still.

A small smile began to form at the corner of his mouth. These kinds of questions were good.

"I'm fine, LeeAnn. I can go to work for another company, if I want." He shrugged. "And I've got enough set aside that I don't have to work for a while, even with Dad's bills."

She waved toward his phone. "What am I supposed to do with all that money?"

The smile turned into a full-fledged grin. "Absolutely anything you want. Start your own yoga studio. Take in abandoned horses. Pay your taxes, maybe?"

"Why are you doing all this?" She didn't move away from him, but she didn't move any closer, either, and she didn't return his smile.

"Because," he said, his voice suddenly turning rough and hoarse, "I love you, LeeAnn. I about died when I thought you'd taken that jackass back. You deserve better than him."

She blinked, processing his words. "Jackass? You mean Darrell?"

Jonah couldn't help but notice that she hadn't responded to his declaration of love. His stomach twisted, but he ran a hand through his hair and kept talking. "Hell, you probably deserve better than me. But you won't find anyone who loves you more than I do." He stopped and waited for her response.

When there was none, he grasped both her hands in his, gazing down at her intently. "But for this to work, you're going to have to trust that I have your best interests at heart—you'll have to trust *me*. I will never, ever do anything to hurt you."

There was a long pause, as LeeAnn stared at him with

solemn gray eyes. "Do you mean it?" she finally asked.

"Absolutely." He nodded, his grin returning.

An answering smile lifted the corner of her lips.

And then she was launching herself into his arms. He crushed her against him, his lips tracing her face, her neck, her mouth.

"Wait," she said, pulling back a little. "Why on earth would you think I had taken Darrell back?" Lines furrowed her brow as she gazed up at him.

"I saw you with him at the Wagon Wheel last week. When I left the paperwork on your car."

Her laughter pealed across the pasture, so loud that the surveyors looked up from their work. "I didn't take him back. I left the diner after I saw you leaving. I tried to follow you."

"You did?" He blinked. A weight he hadn't even known was there lifted from his heart.

"Yes. I wanted to tell you that I wasn't angry you had found the letter. I want Sami and Bev to be happy. I was willing to let Natural Shale drill."

His smile expanded.

"Come on," she said, tugging him toward the house. "Let's go call Sami and Bev and tell them the good news about their share of the magazine money."

"Their share?" He tilted his head.

"Yeah. Someone recently told me that people are more important than things. I figure I'd better put that into practice. Otherwise it's bad karma. It's their inheritance, too."

"I think that sounds like a great idea," he said. "But first, let's tell the survey guys that their work here is done. I've got plans for that field this afternoon."

"Oh, really?" she asked, her tone teasing. "What kind of plans?"

He toed the mat with the tip of his boot. "Think this thing will hold two?"

"Only if they're very, very close." She grinned up at him.

"Oh, I plan to be." He swept her up into his arms and pressed his mouth against hers. "Very close, for a very long time."

She wrapped her arms around his neck and twined her fingers through the thick, dark hair at the nape of his neck. He could feel her smile against his lips as she spoke. "Okay, Superman," she said. "Let's fly."

Epilogue

LeeAnn stepped onto the front porch, admiring Jonah's muscular form as he moved out of Blackie's stable and latched the door behind him. Beside the building, the John Deere tractor was once again running and in regular use.

Jonah spun around and flashed a grin when he caught her staring. "You ready for this?"

A slight shiver ran through her. "Absolutely."

Holding out his hand, Jonah walked slowly toward the path leading to the paddock. LeeAnn caught up with him and slipped her hand into his, marveling at what a difference such a short time could make.

Hard to believe that only a few months ago, I thought he was set to destroy my world.

Instead, he improved everything he touched—*including me.* She smiled at the memory of how they'd spent last night. "Improved" was definitely the right word.

Sami had been right at that barbecue back in the spring.

LeeAnn had never learned to trust anyone. Not until Jonah came along and turned everything she believed upside down.

Well, almost everything.

"Hold on for a minute," she said as they drew close to one of the outbuildings that had housed so many of her gran's hoarded items—now cleaned out, the objects sorted, treasures saved, valuables stored or sold to fund this latest improvement. "I need to grab something."

Pulling open the door, she stepped lightly inside and moved past a small lobby to the back room, where she flipped on a light switch. Tiny fairy lights blazed to life, outlining the mirrors on all the walls. The foam flooring bounced slightly under her feet, and she smiled, remembering the day she had discovered that Jonah had ordered the flooring as a surprise for her. She had stared at it blankly until he told her it was the first part of a renovation he hoped she would let him do on this building.

Her own yoga studio. And they'd built it together.

She'd given her first class in it on Saturday, to Jonah, Sami, Kylie, and Cole. Afterward, they'd all gone out for buttermilk pie at the Wagon Wheel.

Now Jonah was about to help her make another dream come true.

Rummaging through the basket where she kept her keys and shoes when she was inside, she finally found what she'd been looking for and slipped it into her pocket.

"Okay," she said breathlessly when she got outside. "Any word from Sami yet?"

"They're pulling in." Moments later, he swung the new paddock gate open as a truck pulling a horse trailer rolled to a stop in front of it. Sami hopped out of the passenger side and rushed around to the back, opening the trailer gate and murmuring softly.

It was all LeeAnn could do to stop herself from following, but she reminded herself that too much excitement could do more harm than good. When Sami finally appeared again, gently leading a gaunt pinto, tears sprang to LeeAnn's eyes as she watched her cousin guide the animal past the fence that Jonah had spent hours repairing, through the second pasture that they had cleared together, and into the newly patched and freshly painted barn.

A light feeling spun through her, fluttering in her chest and erupting as a quiet, joyful laugh. She walked toward the barn.

"Something funny?" Jonah asked, hooking the gate closed but leaving the lock dangling open.

"Happy," she said with a smile. "There's a lot to do to get a new horse settled—but before we get started, I wanted to give you this."

Reaching into the front pocket of her jeans, she pulled out a melamine keychain, similar to the ones sold in Cowbelles. She started to hand it to him but pulled it back in her fist at the last minute. "I know this isn't really anything big, but I wanted you to have something to always remind you who you are to me."

This time, she dropped it into his hand, surprised by the tiny flutter of anxiety in her stomach.

Jonah stared for a long time at the miniaturized reproduction of the 1953 *TV Guide* cover with George Reeves as Superman. Then, still examining the image, he took the key to the gate out of his shirt pocket and began threading it through the ring.

"The thing is," he said reflectively, "I thought that you decided I was the Henry Cavill Superman."

As she burst into laughter, he wrapped her in his arms and pulled her into a long, slow kiss worthy of any Superman.

Acknowledgments

First of all, thanks to all the readers out there—without you, this book wouldn't exist. Thanks to my family for love, care, and attic space above and beyond the call of duty. You're the best! My eternal gratitude to the BICs, because this would be a lonely endeavor without your support, and to Allison, for teaching me how to write romance. To Pamela: all the love and gratitude for you being you—and for naming TexZen! Special thanks to Melanie for all the last-minute email reads and for introducing me to so many other writers, and to Lateia for knowing I need a finder (and for being the other half of The Plan). Thanks always to the Taylors for being my best friends for so long. As always, to Deb for keeping me connected to this world, even when my head is in the one I'm creating. To The Vampirarchy: you're the best street team an author could ask for. A huge thanks to my editor, Alycia, for responding to my endless questions and email messages with kindness and grace. And to everyone at Entangled: you're amazing. Special thanks to Entangled's copy-editor, proofreader, cover artist, and publicist for making me look good. You're all the best! Any mistakes are my own—and anyone I missed, know that I appreciate you all more than words could ever say.

About the Author

After a decade of moving all around the country (Los Angeles, New York, and Atlanta are a few of the places she's lived), Margo Bond Collins has settled in her native Texas, where she teaches college English courses online and writes contemporary romance, urban fantasy, and paranormal romance. Margo lives near Fort Worth with her daughter and several very spoiled pets, and she spends most of her free time daydreaming about heroes, monsters, cowboys, and villains, and the strong women who love—and sometimes fight—them.

TAMING THE COUNTRY STAR

Country star Cole Grayson is in town, and Kylie Andrews is less than thrilled. As if months of changing the radio station and tearing down his posters weren't bad enough, now she has to deal with a town of fans swarming toward the man who deceived her the year before. Cole is on a mission. After writing a song just for Kylie, he sets off for her hometown to prove he's not the player she thinks he is.